M IS FOR ZOO

By

James David

CHAPTER ONE: BEDTIME!

This should have been an ordinary bedtime for M, but it hadn't been an ordinary day at all, which made this bedtime not very ordinary. M didn't think he would ever get to sleep!

---- **** ----

Earlier that day he'd brushed his teeth and was in his bedroom looking at the photos on his wall. The photos covered the dinosaur wallpaper he had outgrown. He wanted the paper changing, but his Mum had told him he could have it decorated for his tenth birthday. He was nine and a half now, and he couldn't wait to be ten. Not because he wanted to be ten, he was quite happy being nine and a half, but a double figure age was so grown up and he could get rid of the babyish dinosaur wallpaper.

The photos were of his favourite days out with his Mum, Dad and sister. There were photos of them at local parks, some of them at National Trust places and some of them just out shopping. The shopping ones were his sister's idea, she was seven, and she just wanted to use her camera wherever she went. There was even a photo of them in the soup aisle at their local supermarket. What was that all about?

M's favourite photos were of his all-time favourite place to go. The zoo. There were photos of M with animals in the background, of M and his sister Chloe eating ice cream. There was even one where a giraffe had leaned down, right next to him, and almost smiled into the camera. That was his all-time favourite photograph of all time. Chloe thought it was a silly picture. No doubt she'd have preferred one where they were paying for a cauliflower in the supermarket.

He picked up his school clothes from where he'd thrown them the night before, threw them into his laundry basket next to his wardrobe. His shirt and one sock went in. One sock landed on the edge of the basket, and his boxer shorts completely missed and landed on the windowsill. They actually came to rest on the corner of a photograph of him and Chloe at the park. Right on the corner of the photo, the side that Chloe was standing. It looked like she was wearing M's boxers on her head. He laughed to himself, then flicked them into the laundry basket.

M wasn't his real name, and people didn't call him M because they couldn't remember his name and were saying 'erm'. His full name was Maxwell, which he hated, and he didn't like the shortened Max. He'd hadn't liked his name for as long as he could remember. He often wondered if he'd ever liked it, even when he hadn't even been able to talk as a baby. Perhaps he'd pulled a face when one of his grandparents or an auntie had said, "Who's a clever Maxwell then", when he'd sat up for the first time.

Teeth brushed, uniform on and laundry tidied, he headed out of his bedroom and pulled the door shut behind him, leaving his photos and his un-made bed behind. He didn't like his uniform anymore. His white shirts were too tight around the collar, his grey trousers were too short in length and he had a hole in one knee, patched where his Mum had tried to mend them. He'd obviously grown since the start of school last September. It was the end of July, and soon both he and Chloe would be breaking up from school for six weeks. His Mum told him he couldn't have a new uniform so close to the summer holidays. She had said that he'd have outgrown them before school started again next September. So, tight shirts and short patched pants had been M's uniform for the last couple of weeks.

M went into the bathroom. He'd done his teeth, washed his face and hung his towel up like a good boy. He looked in the mirror that hung above the towel rail. His auburn hair wasn't just how he liked.

"Mum?" he shouted, "MUM??"

"Yes?" came the faint reply from downstairs.

"Where's my hair wax?" he shouted again.

"I've got it in my room", came a louder higher pitched reply, this time from upstairs.

There was no answer from downstairs, but that didn't matter. Chloe came into the bathroom with a small blue and white plastic tub. The screw lid was missing, and it was almost empty.

"That was almost full, where's all my hair wax?", said M sternly to Chloe.

Eventually a voice from on the stairs called, it was Mum "Have you found it?".

Chloe waggled her finger beckoning M to follow her.

"I've found the jar it was in", M shouted so his Mum would hear him. Then he heard a sigh from Mum. She had got halfway up the stairs, then sighed as she had to go back down again.

M followed Chloe out of the bathroom to her bedroom, and shock horror, there was all his hair wax. One teddy had a Mohican hair style, one had the fur on its ears all pointy, and poor dolly had so much in her long blonde hair she could have gone to a dolly fancy dress party as a candle. M looked at the toys in disbelief.

"What have you done?" he asked exasperated.

"I had a hairdressing party; do you like them?" Chloe answered proudly.

"I didn't like them before, and I like them even less now", said M.

He looked back into the jar. There was probably just enough for today, but not for the rest of the week, and it was only Tuesday. He went back into the bathroom, leaving Chloe still looking proud of her hairdressing handy work.

As he faced the mirror again, he shouted, sounding quite annoyed, "Mum, Chloe's used all my hair wax on her toys".

Mum obviously hadn't heard him correctly because she answered, "Of course it's for boys", then she added, "It's for anyone, well anyone except your Dad". What she meant was that M's Dad didn't have any hair. Well, he did but he always had it cut very short, so you couldn't tell he was going bald. At least that's what he thought.

M managed to get as much wax as he could from the jar and style his hair just the way he liked it. Dad said M looked like Tin-Tin. M had no idea who Tin-Tin was, until his Dad had shown him a picture on his phone. He was right, but that didn't matter because M looked thought he looked rather cool.

Downstairs Mum had got the school bags ready, washed up, filled drinks bottles and put them with the bags near the front door. Dad had already left for the day but had left a note for M and Chloe as he always did when he had to leave for work early. Both M and Chloe had read their notes whilst eating their breakfast. Chloe's note had read, "Have a fab day princess, love you", and there were three kisses. M's note was a little longer. Dad had read something on his news feed on his phone that he thought would interest M. His note read, "Have a good day M, love you. PS. There is something going on at to zoo. Tell you later", and there were three kisses for him too.

"What's the news about the zoo", M asked his Mum. Mum was flying about the house getting herself and her lunch ready for work, making all sorts of noise.

"Be quick and don't forget to flush" came Mum's reply. She obviously hadn't heard him properly, again!

The day couldn't have gone any slower for M. He needed to know the news about the zoo! After all it was one of his favourite places to go, and one of his favourite photos was of him at the zoo with the giraffe. Although it was only Tuesday, the day seemed to go so slow. It had taken that long to get to lunchtime, it felt like it was Thursday. He had all the afternoon to go yet, then he had to go home, and then he had to wait for his Dad to come home. This was going to be the longest day ever in the history of the world, even since before he was born!

"Dad's home shouted Mum" from the kitchen.

M was upstairs in Chloe's room scraping hair wax out of dolly's matted blonde locks, then trying to get it back in the plastic jar. Dolly's hair was probably ruined anyway, so he couldn't make it any worse. By now Dolly's hair was sticking out straight behind her head. If M held her up, it looked like he was holding her in a very strong wind. He laughed to himself. He heard Mum shout, and dropped Dolly, who flopped to the floor, but her hair stayed exactly the same.

"Hiya M, how was your day?" asked Dad smiling, obviously pleased to see M.

"Long", replied M, out of breath from running down the stairs.

Dad always told him & Chloe not to run down the stairs, because one day they'll come down faster than they'd like. He meant they'd fall. This was an emergency though. "What's the zoo news Dad?" asked M urgently.

"Ofph... Let me get in the house", replied Dad mimicking M's breathlessness.

"Let me take my shoes off, get a drink, and I'll tell you all about it", said Dad.

M huffed and puffed because he'd had a long day waiting all through school, and now his Dad was making him wait even longer.

"Hiya Daddy", came the high pitched tone of Chloe.

"Not now!", said M to Chloe rather sharply, and then continued "Let him get in, take his shoes off and get a drink".

"Hello Princess", replied Daddy to Chloe.

No thought M, please don't let Chloe start a conversation with Dad, otherwise he'd have to wait even longer for the zoo news. He'd already waited forever, and he couldn't wait any longer!!

Meanwhile, back at bedtime, M was in his room, pyjama shorts on, no top as it was a warm evening. His hair was still damp from having just had a cool shower. He was looking through a photo album that his Mum had made him, flicking through all the pictures of him at the zoo. Although his all-time favourite photo of all time was on his wall, he did have other favourites in the album. These were mainly of him with Mr. Stenson, the owner of the zoo and some of the animals. In one of the photos M, Mr. Stenson and a tame chimp were all smiling together. Mr. Stenson was in the middle with M on the left and the tame chimp on the right. Under the photo, M had written, "Me, Mr. Stenson and Charlie the chimp" in his neatest handwriting.

Mr. Stenson was one of the nicest grown up people that M knew, and he knew a lot of grown up people. He was always smiling, and always wore a beige ranger's hat with a green zoo badge on it, green trousers and a green shirt. His sleeves were always rolled up. Mr. Stenson had told M that he didn't like sleeves on shirts, and if he couldn't wear a short sleeved shirt, then his long sleeves had to be rolled up. Under his hat he had longish brown hair with a bit of grey. He had taken over the zoo about five years ago. M remembers his Dad telling him how Mr. Stenson had lots of money, how he loved animals, loved children, and so decided to buy the zoo and make it just for children. M had been a couple of times with school on field trips. M didn't know why they called them field trips, because not once had they ever been to visit a field. He'd thought long and hard about this and decided that visiting a field would not be very interesting at all. He'd almost always chose the zoo over a field any day.

M's best visits were with his Mum, Dad and Chloe, although Chloe was a pain most of the time because she got tired so quickly. She always got tired out before M did. M thought this was because she was a girl, but his Mum said it was because she was younger than he was. Every time they'd visit Mr. Stenson's face would light up. He knew M loved the zoo, and he always treated M like a VIP. M liked that, although when he was first called a VIP, he thought it was a nickname and didn't like it very much. Then he found out it meant Very Important Person, and that made him feel much better about it. He must have been to the zoo every month for the last three years, except when they went on holiday to Spain or somewhere. They didn't go those months, but M never got tired of it, so much so that he wanted to be a zookeeper there when he grew up. Chloe just made fun of him, and the name. She had come home from school once and shouted at the top of her lungs, "I'M JUST GOING FOR A VIP!". When Chloe had finished M questioned her about it, and where she'd been, she answered, "I've been for a VIP, a Very Important Poo!". She was so infuriating at times!!

As he looked at the photos, he couldn't believe what his Dad had told him. The zoo, M's favourite place was closed!! How could this be? M asked himself this over and over, but he didn't have an answer. Only Mr. Stenson had the answer. M had asked his Dad when he'd broken the news, but even Dad didn't have the answer.

"I have no idea", his Dad had said. "Perhaps it's just got too much for him", his Dad continued, obviously talking about Mr. Stenson.

M thought about this, Mr. Stenson, and all the zookeepers. He still didn't know Mr. Stenson's first name. That was ok though, he didn't need to know it, Mr. Stenson knew M's name, and more importantly he knew to call him M, and that made him feel special.

"Hello M", he would say with his huge smile beaming, "Nice to see you here again". It was especially good when M took a mate from school with him. Mr. Stenson greeted him by name but didn't know his friend's name. Mr. Stenson would ask, although he never remembered. He always remembered M's name though!

M climbed into bed, exhausted from his extra-long day and a good half hour of thinking about the zoo closing. As the news gradually sank into M's tired brain, he realised he was getting sadder and sadder. He almost cried, and then he did. He cried quietly at first, then it got louder and louder as he got more and more upset. He was suddenly startled into stopping crying when his bedroom door burst open, and Mum & Dad almost fell over each other to get into his room.

"Is everything alright?", asked his Mum

"What's up, are you hurt?", asked Dad

They said them together, but M heard both questions, not as clearly as them asking separately, but he heard them.

"I'm Fine", M started, but was quickly interrupted by Chloe entering the room. "Why's M crying?", she asked.

M was a little embarrassed, he clearly wasn't fine, but on Dad's advice took a deep breath and explained, "I don't want the zoo to close, it's my favourite place to go in the whole wide world".

"You're a VUP", exclaimed Chloe, which M ignored.

By now both Mum and Dad were sat on either side of M on his bed, each had an arm round him, and M had his head on Mum's shoulder. Chloe didn't like being ignored, so she thought it best to sing. "You're a VUP. You're a VUP. You're a VUP VUP VUP!", and then laughed at herself. No one else was laughing, particularly M.

"Do you even know what a VUP is?", asked Chloe annoyingly.

M just shook his head. He didn't want to answer, partly because he didn't know, partly because he didn't want to know, and partly because he knew Chloe wanted some of the attention he was getting from Mum and Dad.

"It's a Very Upset Person", explained Chloe.

Mum was the first to congratulate Chloe with a "That's really clever darling", followed by an "Oh wow" from Dad. Then Mum added, "I need to put that in your school diary for your teacher to see". M then realised all the attention he was getting for being upset had turned to praise for Chloe for changing the word important in VIP to upset in VUP. M tried not to retaliate, but then couldn't help blurting out, "Well you're a VAP!", sniffled M, "A Very Annoying Person". He felt better, but didn't get the same praise as Chloe, instead they all laughed. All except for M that is.

Eventually everyone left M alone in his room. He looked at the photos again on his wall. "Where will he go now for great days out?", he thought to himself. "What will Mr. Stenson do with all the animals?", was another rather important question he needed an answer to. How could he find out? He had to go to the zoo to ask Mr. Stenson these questions as only he would know the answers for sure.

That just lead to another dilemma though, how could he get to the zoo? He couldn't go on his own, he was nine and a half. The zoo was a fifteen minute drive away. He couldn't walk as he wasn't sure of the way on foot. Besides fifteen minutes in a car might take two days to walk. If it was closed his Mum & Dad wouldn't take him for a day out. There would be no point. They'd either just say no, or they'd drive him to the zoo gates, show him the gates were closed and locked and drive home again. Even worse, they'd ask Chloe where she wanted to go, and he'd end up wasting a whole day of his life on something Chloe wanted to do. He needed a plan. The more M thought, the more M got tired, the more his eyes got heavy. Eventually sleep came and M was heading towards dreamland.

That's how Tuesday turned out to be not very ordinary. It was the longest day ever in the history of M's world, and his favourite zoo was closed. While he slept, he dreamed about many things, all of which he wouldn't remember in the morning.

Wednesday morning was the same routine as yesterday morning. Wake up, breakfast, brush teeth, wash face and get dressed for school. It was while he was buttoning his shirt, staring at his wall of photos, that a plan came into his head. It was an ace plan, almost like he'd spent all night wide awake hatching. He buttoned his shirt faster, found socks, but his school tie was missing. Why whenever he had something important to attend to did one item of school clothing go missing. It could be socks or shoes, it might be a jumper or his PE bag. Today it was his tie. It was as if someone or something knew there was something important to do, and that someone or something decided it might be funny to hide something. M tried to think logically.

"If I was someone or something that wanted to stop someone doing something important, where would I hide something to make them have to waste time looking for it?" he thought to himself.

He shouted from his room, hoping he would be heard, "Dad? What time are you leaving for work?" There was no answer. M hoped he hadn't left yet. Again, he called out, "Mum? Where's my school tie?"

"Because it's Wednesday and you have to go to school, that's why", came back the reply.

M rolled his eyes, mis-heard again.

"Has Dad left for work yet?" he called, still in his room stood still hoping that his tie would miraculously jump out from wherever it was hiding and shout "T-Daaa!".

"No, it's not wet, but I'm hoping it will rain today. The garden needs it" shouted back his Mum.

M let out a huge sigh, he really didn't know why he hadn't learnt by the age of nine and a half that if he shouted anything from upstairs to downstairs or the other way around, his Mum always mis-heard him. M thought he'd take one last look in his wardrobe for his tie. Low and behold there was his tie on the door handle.

"Well that wasn't there before" he muttered under his breath.

He threw it round his neck, he'd tie it properly later, and raced to the stairs. In his head he could hear his Dad telling him not to run down the stairs. He walked quickly, almost running down the stairs to the kitchen.

In the kitchen, Chloe was sat at the table tucking into her chocolate rice cereal. Mum was preparing herself and her lunch for work. She was a librarian's assistant. Not at the local library where they were members, but at a University library. M had never been there, but he imagined the books were a lot bigger and thicker than any books he'd ever seen. She always took a packed lunch to work with her. "It saves me having to go out for my lunch" she'd say. M supposed that assisting a librarian with giant books all day must be tiring, so the last thing you'd want to do would be to go out for lunch.

M had entered the kitchen from the lounge, and opposite that door was another door that lead to the cloak room, and from there, through a door on the right, you could get into the garage.

The kitchen was sort of split into two, a cooking part and an eating part, although the eating part also doubled as the homework part. M preferred it when it was the eating part. To the left of where M had entered, past the table on your right, which was in the middle of the eating part, was the cooking part. That's where Mum was, and probably had something to do with why she always misheard anyone calling from upstairs. She never said pardon though, she always answered what she thought had been asked. M's breakfast was on the table, he just needed milk from the fridge. The fridge was on the opposite side of the kitchen right in the middle of the cooking and eating parts. He opened the fridge door; Dad came in from the garage. As M closed the door, he was startled to see his Dad there and almost dropped the milk.

"I'm not that scary am I", Dad joked. M smiled, "I'm so glad you haven't left yet", exclaimed M, "I need to talk to you about the zoo". "Well I've got ten minutes before I have to leave, so wassuuuuup", said Dad in a silly voice. M tried to cram in as much concern, consideration and emotion, and as many words as he could think of within that ten minutes.

"Why is the zoo closed? Has it closed already? What's Mr. Stenson going to do? What about all the animals? Who is going to look after them? Who will feed them and clean their enclosures? What if they get sick? Mr. Stenson loved his zoo and everyone who came to see the animals. What's going to happen", said M sort of all at once.

"Woah Woah, slow down", said Dad

"But Dad", M continued, "The zoo can't just close!"

"Ok", said Dad, trying to reassure M, "I'm sure the animals will be fine. I know that Mr. Stenson loved animals, and he loved children going to see them. I know he loved to see you there", he said smiling at M. "I'm sure that if it has to close, there must be a very good reason."

"But that's just it Dad, I can't think of any good reason why Mr. Stenson would just close the zoo if he loved it so much", M said very emphatically.

"I don't have any answers for you I'm afraid". He could see the genuine concern on M's face and felt a bit guilty.

"We need to find out", implored M.

At that moment, Mum opened the back door that lead into the garden. Once the door was open no one could hear anyone because of the dog from next door barking loudly. It was a big dog, although no one was quite sure of the breed, but it had a big dogs bark. M had asked Mrs Spooner once what breed it was, but he couldn't remember. Mrs Spooner was their neighbour whose dog it was. He knew it was one of those funny breeds like a Labra-Doodle. Was it a Springer-sation or a King Russell? Dad always said she got it from a farm, and it was a sheep dog crossed with a duck, and it was called a Collie-Waddle. It wasn't, and it did look like a collie.

"Oh blimey", exclaimed Dad, "The sooner Mrs Spooner takes her Collie-Waddle to that dog behaviour specialist, the better".

"They come to her", Mum said without looking up from what she was doing, "Every day"

"Not doing a very good job, are they?" replied Dad.

Mum added, "I seem to remember she was using an animal hypnotist to calm it down"

"Still not doing a very good job are they?". As he said this he winked, smiling at M, who was now sat at the table eating his breakfast.

Mrs. Spooner wasn't the best of neighbours. She didn't speak much, and never smiled whenever M or Chloe saw her out and about. In fact Mrs. Spooner had become quite a miserable person. She would cross the road whenever they were about to pass on the same pavement. She would ignore them if they saw her whilst out shopping in the town. If ever a ball accidentally went over the hedge into her garden, they would never get it back. M and Chloe, and Mum and Dad for that matter had tried to knock on her door when a ball had gone over. Mrs. Spooner had always pretended not to be in, even though she knew she was. They had even seen her with her dog on the park playing with one of their balls.

She wasn't a very nice neighbour at all. Just as well they hadn't seen her for a while.

Safe to say, all they knew about Mrs. Spooner, how miserable she was, and she had a dog that barked incessantly. She wasn't married, and they didn't know if she ever had been. She wore old clothes and her hair was always scruffy. Mum always said she looked like she'd been dragged through a hedge sideways, and Dad always said she probably made the hedge apologise.

"And with that, I must be off" said Dad. He went to the cooking part, and gave Mum a kiss and a hug, kissed Chloe on his way back to the garage door. He hugged M and gently ruffled his hair as he left, the looked at his hand.

"Ewww, hair wax!"

M had a mouthful of chocolate crispies which he tried to chew and swallow before Dad could reach the garage door. He succeeded.

"But what about the zoo Dad?" M asked desperately.

"We'll talk about it after school", replied Dad, closing the door behind him. "See you all later", they heard him say as the door closed.

M sighed a huge sigh. "That's another day I've got to wait". He thought he'd said this to himself in his head, until his Mum said, "Got to wait for what?" M was surprised at the question. "Until I can find out more about Mr. Stenson and the zoo" he told her.

"Can I have some toast?", requested Chloe quite out of the blue.

M pushed his cereal bowl towards the centre of the oblong table and with elbows on the table dropped his head into his hands. He let out another big sigh. Once again Chloe had taken all the focus from M and the zoo to something far more important. Toast!!

Wednesday's school day came and went. There were no dramas or dilemmas, except of course in M's head. Not one person, a pupil, a teacher or a lunchtime assistant, not anyone mentioned anything about the zoo being closed. M couldn't believe it wasn't important to anyone except him, but without knowing the reason, he didn't want to mention it. He was going to race home hoping Dad would be back early so they could spend some time talking about it alone without Chloe interrupting or making silly comments or asking for stupid things, like food.

Chloe was picked up from school by Mum, but M preferred to walk home. Sometimes he'd walk with his friends, sometimes alone, but always straight home. It wasn't a long walk; it could take M ten minutes to walk home quickly. On a day when he'd walk with friends it could take twenty five minutes because they'd be chatting and dawdling. It was quite safe as there were no really busy main roads, and the one slightly busy road had a lollipop lady crossing the children over. All the children thought she was quite funny. Well she wasn't funny, but her name was. Mrs Cross. Mum would always say, "Be careful on the way home", and M would reply, "I'll cross with Mrs. Cross".

As M walked towards the junction, he could see Mrs. Cross' lollipop poised in the upright position. She was mid cross and the last of the people she'd just crossed was stepping up the kerb. M saw the lollipop lower slightly as Mrs. Cross made her way back to the pavement where M was heading. She saw M as she stepped up the kerb on this side.

"Good afternoon young man", she said to M in that really friendly voice she had. She was probably a little older than his Mum, but not as old as his Nana. Every time M crossed the road with her, she always had her thick red hair in a ponytail.

"Hello Mrs Cross", replied M, "How are you?".

"I'm very well thank you for asking"

Mrs. Cross used to work with M's Mum in another library, not where his Mum worked now. They had remained good friends and now and again M would have to pass messages on from one to the other. Sometimes the messages would make sense, and sometimes M wouldn't have a clue what they meant. She knew M and he knew her.

"What's all this about your favourite zoo being closed?"

M stopped in his tracks, and just stared at Mrs. Cross. "You know about the zoo?" asked M.

"Of course I know", replied Mrs. Cross, "It was one of my favourite places too", she told M. "I can remember when it was first opened, I was one of the first visitors. I worked with Mr. Stenson for a few years before he had the zoo", she told M.

M was astounded at this news. He never knew Mrs. Cross knew Mr. Stenson, but why would he? He never really had a conversation with Mrs. Cross, he just passed messages on to her from his Mum and back again and crossed the road with her.

M had forgotten that he was on his way home from school, and more importantly he had forgotten he was in a hurry. Mrs. Cross had seen to that with her gob-smacking news.

"I don't understand it really" said Mrs. Cross to M, and she went on, "I spoke to Mr. Stenson not so long ago, and he never said anything". At that moment there was a loud coughing sound from the other side of the road, "Ah-Hem!".

As well as M forgetting he was on his way home, and in a hurry, Mrs. Cross had momentarily forgotten she was the school crossing patrol. She looked towards the coughing and with a bit of a jump said, "Oh! I'm so sorry", then to M she said, "Wait for my signal". With that she looked both ways to make sure it was safe to step into the road with her lollipop. M waited, then took the nod from Mrs. Cross as the safe to cross signal. As M passed her, she said, "Wait on the kerb for me please". Immediately M thought she would have a message for him Mum to pass on. As the other people crossed, Mrs. Cross was saying, "Sorry about the wait" to them. Once everyone was safely on the opposite sides of the road from where they'd started, Mrs. Cross made her way to the kerb, and to M.

"I'm really sad about the zoo", M told Mrs Cross, "It really was my favourite place to go".

"I can see you're sad", Mrs Cross replied, and then in a consoling manner said, "I'm sure it's something and nothing".

"I don't agree" said M passionately. This took Mrs. Cross aback a little. She obviously wasn't expecting to be disagreed with, and this showed on her face.
"S..s..sorry, I didn't mean to be rude", M said apologetically as he saw the look Mrs. Cross' was expressing.

"Nonsense" said Mrs. Cross, "I wasn't expecting that, I was expecting a grunt or a shrug of your shoulders", she explained.

M smiled at her. "I'd better be getting home", said M, "I need to speak to my Dad a bit more about it".

It was Mrs. Cross' turn to smile at M. "Soon be end of term young man, last day tomorrow. It can all be sorted out in the summer holidays", she told M. Off M went, with the original speed he'd had before he'd crossed with Mrs. Cross.

When M turned the corner of Windermere Road into his road, the first thing he saw was Dad's car on the drive. They lived in the second house along on the right. This made M walk the last few metres to his house even faster. Up the drive, passed the car, and into the garage. He entered the kitchen by the same door his Dad had left through that morning. As he entered, he entered into the homework part. It was always the homework part before it was the eating part. Then he remembered it was the last week of school and there was no homework. That was cause for a sigh of relief from M.

Dad was sat at the table with his laptop open and was busy typing.

"Hi Dad", M said. No response. "Had a good day Dad?" M enquired.

Again, there was no response. M walked around the table, so he was facing his Dad. Dad looked up and jumped, then took out his ear plugs.

"Blimey, you frightened me", said Dad smiling.

"Sorry", M apologised, but all he had done was walk in his own house.

M smiled back, then laughed. Dad jumping was quite amusing.

"I just need to finish this", said Dad still typing, "Give me ten minutes".

M sighed again and took his school backpack into the cloak room to hang up and set a mental timer for exactly ten minutes. As he walked towards the kitchen door again the garage door opened, and in walked Chloe, followed by Mum.

"Hello darling", Mum said to M, "Did you have a good day?".

"Yes thanks", replied M following Chloe and Mum into the kitchen.

"What's for tea?" asked Chloe.

"It's gammon tonight", Mum told her.

"I don't like gammon!", complained Chloe.

That was another thing that annoyed M about Chloe. Whatever they were having to eat, Chloe always complained she didn't like it. Even though when it was put in front of her, she would eat it, enjoy it and ask for more. Like last night, they had sausage rolls with chips and salad. Chloe ate all hers up then asked for more sausage roll, but when she was told what they were having, Chloe had complained she didn't like sausage rolls. She was a right pain.

It had been about seven minutes by M's mental timer, so his Dad had three minutes left to finish what he was doing.

"There's drinks on the table" Mum shouted, which she did every afternoon after school. M picked up his cup. He knew it was his cup because it had the remains of an M on the side of it. He'd had the same cup for as long as he could remember. As he drank his apple juice he watched to see if Dad was anywhere near finishing whatever he was doing.

"Are you nearly done Dad?" M asked his expectantly.

"Two more minutes, then I have a phone call to make", came the reply.

Dad didn't even look up from his computer when he answered. Another sigh from M, although his mental timer hadn't gone off yet. Then Dad, closed his laptop up, smiled to himself, and went straight to the phone that was laying on the table.

M looked at his Dad almost willing the phone to fly out of his hand so that the call couldn't happen. M desperately wanted to talk about the zoo. Dad dialled and M could hear the faint sound of the ringing tone from the phone as it wasn't to his Dad's ear yet. Then he heard it stop. Dad put the phone to his ear, about to talk and then, "Funny", said Dad puzzled.

"What's funny?" M asked.

"Hold on, I'll try again", said Dad.

He dialled the number again and this time put the phone straight to his ear. He let it ring five times, then again took the phone from his ear. "Very odd", said Dad putting the phone back on the table. M assumed it was a work call, so didn't ask again.

"Dad?" said M, wanting to start a conversation.

"Is everything ok darling?" asked Mum looking at Dad's puzzled face.

"I just tried calling Mr. Stenson at the zoo" Dad told her. M's ears pricked up, "But the phone was cut off", said Dad, still puzzled.

"Maybe there's no one there to answer", reasoned Mum.

Dad's puzzled look was still on his face. "No", he said, "The phone was picked up, then someone put the phone down, the call wasn't just rejected", continued Dad. "Maybe they're fed up of calls just now. I'll try again in a few days", Dad concluded.

"I think something is wrong", said M in his most business like voice.

"Something and nothing most likely", comforted Dad. That's what Mrs. Cross had said.

M wasn't convinced, and he suspected neither was Dad.

CHAPTER TWO: MRS. CROSS TO THE RESCUE

The following morning, Thursday, was the last day of school. M thought and probably had dreamed of nothing but the zoo. Although he never remembered his dreams, he presumed he'd most likely dreamed of nothing else. Up, dressed, teeth brushed, and hair styled, and all in record time, M went downstairs to get his breakfast. Mum was in the cooking part of the kitchen again and looked up as M came in.

"Haven't you forgotten something this morning?", she asked.

M checked himself, trousers, shirt, socks. As far as he was concerned, he was ready to eat breakfast and get off to school. He felt his collar. His tie! He had forgotten his tie. He turned to go back upstairs when he noticed Chloe at the table. She was always first down for breakfast, and today was no different, although she looked different. No school uniform!!

Chloe smiled at M and said, "You've forgotten it's non uniform day, haven't you?"

M realised his mistake and continued out of the kitchen back upstairs. He quickly changed into a pair of checked shorts and a t-shirt. He left the now redundant school uniform on the floor in his room. He'd tidy that up later. He made his way back downstairs, and met Mum coming up.

"I hope you've put that uniform away", she said to M.

He turned on the stairs and went back to his room to do as he was asked or rather told.

Then he heard his Mum shout, "And don't leave before I've given you a message for Mrs Cross".

The message to Mrs. Cross was one of those he couldn't make head nor tail of. M liked the plain straight forwards ones better. He preferred messages like, "I'll meet you tomorrow at the café on the high street" or "Come around for coffee after work", you know, easy ones. He could remember them. Today's message wasn't one of those, and it wouldn't stay in his head.

"Tell Mrs. Cross", Mum said, "It starts at seven and red is fine as long as it's not too big. Do you want me to write it down?" she asked.

"I'll be fine", replied M, and repeated, "It starts at seven and red is fine as long as it's not too big. Got it!" he convinced Mum. M went away to finish getting ready for school. "I'm not taking a coat Mum, it's a blue sky", he told her.

"Take a jumper though M", replied Mum.

"Do I need a coat?", piped up Chloe.

"No, just a jumper like M", said Mum back to her.

"It starts at seven, and red is fine as long as it's not too big", said M out loud, partly to reassure himself he'd got it right, and partly or mostly to reassure Mum he had it right.

"Perfect!" said Mum reassured.

"It starts with red and seven will be too big but it's fine", mimicked Chloe.

"Now don't confuse matters, Chloe", said Mum.

Just then Dad appeared from the garage door, "What's big and red and starts at seven?" he said as soon as he entered the kitchen.

"Don't you start confusing things either", said Mum laughing. Both M and Chloe laughed too.

It was time to leave for school. M got his bag on his shoulder. Although he had no books to take as it was the last day, he did have a present and a card for Miss Rawson his teacher. Likewise, Chloe also had a present and a card for her teacher Mrs. Metcalfe. Mum had chosen both presents especially. She knew teachers, being a librarian at a university, and she knew they hated to receive 'tat' at the end of the school year. M made his way to the garage door.

"Bye Mum, bye Dad. Love you both".

Mum was having none of that, "Excuse me", she said in her best teacher like voice, "You may be leaving year three, but you can still give your Mum a kiss in the morning". M just smiled and went to her to deliver a kiss and an "I love you", before he left.

"See you at school Chloe", he said as he walked towards the door again.

"Errm, excuse me", said Dad in a silly teacher voice, "You might be going into year four next year, but you can still give your Dad a hug and a high five".

M smiled at his Dad and complied with Dad's request. Then he left through the door shouting, "It starts at seven, and red is fine as long as it's not too big".

As M walked through the garage towards the driveway, he noticed a small van parked outside Mrs. Spooner's next door. It was a white van with silhouettes of animals stuck onto it. M could make out a dog, a cat, a rabbit and a, well he had no idea what that one was, but it looked like a bird of some sort. Maybe a parrot? Possibly. There was a pale blue cloud-like shape on the side and on the single back door of the van, which read, "Sue McQueen – Animal Behaviour Therapist" and a phone number surrounded by little footprints of the different animals.

"This must be the one Mum was talking about that came to stop Mrs. Spooner's dog from barking", he thought to himself. Then he smiled as he imagined a sign on the car saying, "Specialists in collie-waddles", which is what his Dad said Mrs Spooner's dog was. He turned left out of his drive, and the walk to school had commenced properly.

M walked his usual route to school. As he passed the row of shops, he saw other kids from another school at the bus stop. He was glad he didn't have to take the bus.

"Hi M", came a shout from one of his friends, James. M waved back and continued his walk. Eventually he could see the crossing, and just above a tallish hedge he could see the top of Mrs. Cross' lollipop. He recited the message in his head to make sure he had it right. He turned the corner, and said in his best good morning voice, "Morning Mrs. Cross, I've got a message from Mum. It starts at seven, and red is fine as long as it's not too big".

Mrs. Cross turned to M, and looked at him blankly, "Morning M, sorry, what was that?"

"It starts at seven, and red is fine as long as it's not too big", he repeated, "A message from Mum".

"Oh lovely, thanks M", Mrs. Cross replied with a smile.

M was hoping she'd shed some light on its meaning, but she didn't. Then with the same smile she continued, "Last day M? Any plans for the holidays?"

M just shrugged, "I don't think so", he told her, "I think Dad's working, Mum's got some time off, and we're going to our grandparents sometimes".

Then he remembered, if the schools were on holiday, who would Mrs. Cross have to cross. With that he asked, "What are you doing when the schools are closed?"

What she replied with hit M like a massive Nerf gun bullet, "Well first thing tomorrow, I'm off to see my friend Mr. Stenson at the zoo, to see what all this closing is about. I called him yesterday, but the call was disconnected. To see if there's anything I can do".

M wanted to go with her, he needed to go with her. "Like someone answered and put the phone down? Can I come with you?". Once again that was a question he had in his head, but somehow his tongue had got hold of it and blurted it out of his mouth.

"Yes, just like someone putting the phone down, how did you know?", she asked inquisitively.

"Because that's what happened when my Dad called the zoo", said M emphatically.

"I'm not sure you can come with me", said Mrs. Cross, "Have you asked your Mum?".

M thought about saying yes, but that would have been a lie, so he didn't. "I haven't", said M honestly, but I will when I get home. Please can I come with you?" he pleaded.

Mrs. Cross could see the desperation in his face. "Tell you what", she said, "I'll call your Mum later today and we'll talk about it". M smiled, but not a big smile, just a hopeful smile.

"Thanks Mrs. Cross", he said with the same hopeful smile.

"Right, we need to get you to school". With that, she looked both ways, and stepped into the road to cross M over.

At school M could think of little else but going to the zoo with Mrs. Cross. He hoped and hoped that his Mum would say he could go.

As it was the last day of school, no proper work was being done. Some children had brought games in, some were allowed in the IT suite on a rota basis to play games on the iPads and some were choosing to sit on the fields in groups just relaxing. Those on the fields were mainly the year sixes that were leaving for high school. M was too preoccupied in his thoughts to concentrate on anything for long. He was like a bee jumping from flower to flower. One minute he was in the library, then in the IT suite, but he left there even before his time slot was finished. He went back to his classroom to join in the board games, but he got bored quickly. He knew some year six kids, so he went to sit on the field chatting. He found himself daydreaming and unable to keep up with the conversations, so he moved somewhere else. Eventually he was roaming around the school looking like he was going somewhere, but actually going nowhere.

Before long it was lunch time, and that was completely uneventful, except it seemed that the cook was blatantly having a clear out. He had never seen so much choice. There was fish fingers, chicken goujons, quiches, tomato pasta, cheesy pasta. There was also a huge range of desserts, yoghurts, flapjacks, cookies, fruit salad, whole fruit. Unlike most days, there was a sign that said, "All you can eat". M wasn't that hungry, but he knew that he needed to keep his strength up so he could think clearly should he need to. He chose quiche, chips and beans and had fresh fruit and yoghurt for dessert. He chose the fruit salad as it was already prepared and chopped, so he didn't have to mess around with peels, cores and pips. He did leave the mango pieces which he wasn't keen on. He sat at a table on his own at first, but was then joined by Alfie, Theo, Ethan, Izzy and Katie from year six. He knew these as they all lived and played locally. Alfie and Theo had so much it looked like there were no plates, just food piled on their trays.

The afternoon was more of the same, although they had to stay in their own classrooms a reason only known to the teachers and headmaster. M played chess with Ellie and Kayle, but both of them beat him so they weren't very long games. Normally M would have beaten them, and there would only have been time for only one game, but M's mind just wasn't on the job in hand. At one thirty, Miss Rawson clapped her hands.

"One, two, three, look at me". That was her way of getting their attention.

"It's time to put our games away", she announced.

From some of the children there were groans, and from others there were looks of disappointment.

"Then", Miss Rawson continued, "We need to collect all our belongings that we're taking home as school will be finishing at two o'clock today".

The groans were replaced by cheers and the looks of disappointment had turned to smiles. It seemed they'd all forgotten school was finishing early on the last day. Immediately there was an excited hullabaloo of activity as all the children, M included, packed all their toys and games away.

On the way home, the children who walked to and from school were laden with books and games that they were taking and returning to their homes. M's chess set was compact and slipped into his bag easily. He just had a stack of five exercise books he had to carry. M thought this would slow him down, then he remembered he would be meeting Mrs. Cross, who should have spoken to his Mum. This thought made the books seem almost weightless. Two o'clock came and it was the end of school. Goodbyes to teachers and pupils were exchanged, and the school emptied, probably quicker than any other day of the year.

As M approached the crossing, the trees hid any sign of a lollipop, so he could only assume Mrs. Cross was waiting on the pavement at the corner. As he turned the corner, he was smiling ready, expectantly, ready for Mrs. Cross' to return the smile. Shock, horror and a sinking feeling quickly removed his smile as he was greeted by a man holding the lollipop instead.

"Where's Mrs. Cross", M said sharply, completely forgetting his manners.

The lollipop man wasn't very talkative at all. Maybe it was M's attitude that made him not want to chat, or maybe he was just unpleasant. Instead the man just stared at M, waited for another few children to get to the crossing, then walked slowly to the kerb. He waited for a gap in the traffic before stepping into the road and holding the lollipop to the ground like a proud Roman soldier would hold his spear. The last vehicle to go passed was one that M recognised. It was the van he'd seen earlier parked outside Mrs. Spooner's. He thanked the man that had crossed him, who grunted back. Maybe he just wasn't the talkative kind, thought M.

M walked into his short driveway. The garage door was closed, so he had to wait at the front outer porch door for someone to let him in. He'd forgotten that Mum had to pick Chloe up from school. He'd also forgotten that he was supposed to be getting a lift from Mum too. He waited. This had happened before. Mum would wait at the school for both of them, then when she was sure M had forgotten, she'd make her way home. Ten minutes he waited. Mum's car turned the corner and parked outside the house. He could see Mum looking at him, and her head shaking as if to tell M he was a numpty for forgetting. He could see Chloe in the back on her car seat, but he couldn't see who was in the passenger seat. Mum was in the way, well if she hadn't been in the way, nobody would be driving! Once Mum was out of the car and opening the back door to let his sister out, the person in the passenger seat was a smiling Mrs. Cross. M's heart almost leapt out of his chest with excitement.

"Can I go?", shouted M to his Mum.

M wasn't expecting himself to shout like he did, but his mouth started working before his brain gave it permission. Mrs. Cross laughed out loud, and Mum just turned from Chloe to him and shushed him. Only then did M realise how loud he'd shouted. Once Chloe and all her belongings were out of the car, Mum opened the front door, disabled the house alarm and they all filed through the hall, passed the stairs on the right and into the kitchen. Everything, bags, books and jumpers were dumped on the kitchen table.

In the kitchen M was looking frantically from Mrs. Cross to his Mum waiting for one of them to speak or at least for their facial expressions to give him a clue about whether he could go to the zoo with Mrs. Cross or not.

"Can I have a drink please Mummy?", asked Chloe.

"Of course", replied Mum, "Just let's get in and settled. Would you like a drink Jo?" Mum asked Mrs. Cross. "What about you M?"

"I'd love a tea", Mrs. Cross replied, and looked at M. Nothing, nothing on her face gave M any clue. It was like she'd forgotten all about their conversation that morning.

"Can I have an apple juice?". Once again M had forgotten manners, but was quickly reminded when Mum sternly reminded him, "Can I have an apple juice what?"

"Please", added M shyly. He couldn't even look at Mrs. Cross now through embarrassment all though he knew all eyes were on him now.

As the kettle boiled, Mum cleared the kitchen table and instructed M and Chloe, "Bags and books upstairs please, get changed, uniforms in the washing basket, M yours can go in the bin – Then you can have drinks". Both M and Chloe left the kitchen both sighing heavily.

After about ten minutes M returned to the kitchen, closely followed by Chloe and were greeted in the kitchen by the promised drinks waiting for them. Chloe took a sip of hers, then helped herself to an apple from the bowl on the side. She took that and her drink into the other room. Mum and Mrs. Cross were deep in conversation about someone or something or other. M listened secretively, pretending he wasn't, but it was like they were talking in code. They didn't mention anyone's name or any place. M was waiting to hear the word 'zoo' or 'Mr. Stenson' or 'animals', but without names or places it was just code.

"How is a person supposed to overhear a conversation properly if certain facts are deliberately missed out?", he thought to himself. Eventually, he could no longer contain himself. The longer they talked code, the less time they'd have to discuss the zoo. Mrs. Cross would have to leave soon, and that would be the end of his chance to go with her.

"Mum?", he interrupted. He was ignored. "Excuse me Mum?", he attempted again, but this time got a "One minute M", back, who continued with the gibberish to Mrs. Cross. He waited, still listening, still unable to decipher. The question, "Can I go to the zoo with Mrs. Cross" was all that was in his head. He felt like it was getting bigger and bigger and brighter and brighter, and eventually, if he didn't say it, it would get so bright in his brain he would be able to project it onto the white wall at the end of the eating part of the kitchen. Mum and Mrs. Cross would see it then. Oh yes, they would!! Eventually M could no longer keep the question to himself, and it just came out, really loud and really fast.

"Please can I go to the zoo with Mrs. Cross?" M was as shocked as Mum and Mrs. Cross at the volume and speed of his question. He sat wide eyed in astonishment. Mum and Mrs. Cross were silenced by it.

"Sorry!", said M, "I didn't mean to shout", he said apologetically. For a moment M thought he was going to get really told off.

Mum and Mrs. Cross looked at M, then looked at each other, then were helpless with laughter.

Later that evening M was in his room reading, Chloe was downstairs helping Mum with the dinner, as only Chloe could. M heard a car engine and then it stopped. After about a minute or so he heard the garage to kitchen door shut. He could hear it as the door didn't close quite right on its own and had to be pushed shut. This made a wood on wood squeaking sound. Dad was home. M raced out of his room, then carefully, but quickly down the stairs, through the hall and into the kitchen.

"Hi M", came his Dad's voice. Now M was just a ball of excitement, and said, "Mums said I can go to the zoo with Mrs. Cross tomorrow and we're going to find out why its closed and see Mr. Stenson, and ask him what the problem is, and, and...!". Dad interrupted M's flow. "Woah, slow down, take a breath and start again so I can understand you", said Dad smiling. Of course Dad already knew all the details as Mum had discussed it earlier with him on the phone before she had finalised the details with Jo (Mrs. Cross).

M breathed and then started again but a bit slower, "Mrs. Cross is going to the zoo tomorrow to see Mr. Stenson and ask him why he's closed. Mum said I can go with her".

There were of course some conditions that M had omitted, but in his excitement it was excusable. He had to do exactly as Mrs. Cross told or asked him. He had to take a packed lunch. He had to leave when Mrs. Cross told him it was time to leave. He had to make sure he stayed with Mrs. Cross, and if her went anywhere else with anyone else, Mrs. Cross had to know about it. As well as he knew the zoo map off by heart, Mrs. Cross needed to know where he was all the time. M had of course agreed to all the conditions and rules in order that he could go.

"Wow M", said Dad, just as excitedly, "That sounds like a marvellous idea", he continued, making M think that this was all news to him.

"I'm going to find out exactly what's going on", said M to his Dad very matter of factly.

"Well you do that", replied Dad, "And report back to us all your investigative findings", replied Dad just as matter of factly.

"I will", said M, then asked, "What are investagle finings, I mean investing finders, I mean what you said, what are they?".

Dad laughed and repeated, "Investigative findings are what the newspaper and news reporters on the TV get when they're working on a major story".

Bedtime couldn't come fast enough for M that evening. Everything from eating tea after Mrs. Cross had gone home to was brushing his teeth was done at the speed of light. Both Mum and Dad noticed the speed in which he went in and out of the bathroom.

"Did you brush your teeth properly?", asked Dad

"Erm… Yes", replied M

"Erm… No!", Dad replied back, "Back in the bathroom young man and do your teeth again, properly".

When Dad called M 'young man' he knew he was being serious.

M skulked back into the bathroom like a puppy that had been told off for weeing on the kitchen floor.

At last M was in bed. So much sleep to have, so much planning to do. How was he going to fit all that in to one night? He couldn't sleep because he was planning, he couldn't plan because he needed to sleep. He couldn't win. M laid on his side, then his back. He tried to lie on his tummy, then his other side, then on his back again. He sighed on his side, on his tummy, on his back. He even sat up, fluffed his pillows and sighed. It was no good. He wasn't going to get any sleep. Too much excitement and planning. Planning and excitement. He sighed again. Maybe he's gone to bed too early. It was only five to seven. What was it his Nana used to say to him at Christmas?

"If you go to bed early, Christmas comes quicker", she'd say.

CHAPTER THREE: OFF TO THE ZOO

When M woke up, he was on his back and he stared at the ceiling. He yawned, which was different to sighing. He laid there, just staring at the ceiling. He wondered to himself about how long it took him to get to sleep last night. Was it just a matter of minutes, or had it taken an hour and a half? He had no idea. All he knew was that he'd woken up on his back, there was light coming through the gap between his blind and the windowsill. Suddenly he sat bold upright!

"I'M GOING TO THE ZOO!!", his voice shouted in his head.

Had it come out of his mouth at that volume he was sure he would have woken everyone in his house and maybe everyone in his street!!

M jumped out of bed and then checked the time. Maybe he should have checked the time before getting out of bed. Never mind that now, it was ten past seven. M had a horrid thought; he hated the thought when he'd thought it. The last time he looked at the clock it was five to seven. Now it was ten past seven. Maybe he's only been asleep for fifteen minutes. He checked. No, it was morning, and if leaving your bedroom, going downstairs and into the kitchen to get breakfast had been an Olympic event, this morning he would have got a personal best and a gold medal. Mum was already up and had thoughtfully made up a packed lunch for him.

As it was the first day of the summer holidays, Mum had arranged some time off work. She and Dad took turns to take time off, except when they went away on holiday, then they were off together.

"Am I staying all day?", M asked Mum as she was zipping up the picnic bag.

"I presume so", replied Mum, "Mrs. Cross is picking you up around nine thirty, so I don't expect you back before lunch"

"Really?", M questioned in disbelief.

"Can I go?" quizzed Chloe, as she entered the kitchen still half asleep.

"Not really", M told her, "It could be dangerous"

"Then why are you going?", she quizzed further.

Mum intervened at this point, "Mr. Stenson wants to explain everything to M Chloe"

"He does??", asked M. quite surprised, then saw his Mum wink, "Oh yes he does"

"Are you going to be the boss of the zoo then?" asked Chloe. Both M and Mum laughed, which embarrassed Chloe. This made her storm out of the kitchen in a huff shouting "Fine!".

Mum ran after Chloe trying to explain why what she said had been amusing. M decided he'd have a look in the picnic bag to see what he had to look forward to. Inside the picnic bag was a smaller cool bag. There were sandwiches, well it was a bread roll really with Mum's special cheese, ham and onion filling, crisps (ready salted), a banana and a fruit bar. He opened the smaller bag, in it was two cartons of juice, one orange and one apple. Mum had made a mistake as he was only allowed one carton usually.

He shouted to his Mum, "Are both these juices for me?"

Mum answered in her inimitable way, "Well go on then, and don't forget to go before you go out as well".

M rolled his eyes; he hadn't asked if he could go for a pee!! He zipped up the bags and left them where they were. Then he had a brain wave, walking boots or wellies, he thought he might need one or the other. He diverted his attention from picnic bags to footwear that were kept in the garage. M wasn't sure why they called it a garage. Dad had never put his car in there once. He put it half in one time when it was raining, and he used the up and over garage door to shelter the engine. He wasn't doing anything mechanical, he was changing a bulb in the headlights, and didn't want to get soaking wet in the process. But the whole car had never been in the garage. He found the boot box, but there were two pairs missing. A pair of walking boots and a pair of wellies. His boots and wellies to be precise. Where could they be? He couldn't go in his trainers, surely? They'd get ruined. He went back into the house.

By the time he got back into the kitchen Mum was back down downstairs and had his breakfast all ready. Chocolate rice pops with milk and a glass of juice. Apple was his favourite.

"Would you like some toast?", Mum asked.

"Yes please, with blackcurrant jam", M replied between mouthfuls of cereal.

"Has Dad gone to work?" M enquired.

"hmmm Hmmm", replied Mum nodding. She couldn't say yes as she had a mouthful of toast herself.

Mum's mobile beeped, which she picked up before the beeping had stopped. She read whatever was on the screen and smiled. M presumed it was a text from Dad, as Mum started to compose a reply, pressed send and replaced the phone on the work top. She finished her next mouthful and took a sip of tea.

"Mrs. Cross hopes you still want to go out today", she told M, "I've said you do".

It was M's turn to hum his answer of yes and nod vigorously, he actually couldn't wait. Mum's phone beeped again, which she read and smiled again.

"That's what I told her; she says she can't wait either". M smiled through a mouthful of cereal and a dribble of chocolate milk left the corner of his mouth, which he wiped with the back of his hand.

M wondered if when he got a mobile phone of his own for his next birthday, could he text him Mum when she not in the same room. That way she couldn't mis-hear what he said or asked, and he wouldn't get the wrong answer.

M finished his cereal and Mum presented him with some toast, which he devoured very quickly. "Thank you for my breakfast, please may I leave the table?", M asked, as he always did after a meal.

"You may", confirmed Mum.

M was about to move his chair back, when Chloe returned, dressed, coat on and her outfit was completed with the addition of her school backpack.

"I'm coming with you", she said in a very serious manner.

M looked at Chloe in disbelief. This could just ruin his whole day if he had Chloe tagging along behind him. He looked at Mum with the same disbelief, and Mum smiled back at him, with her head to one side. He knew that smile. That smile was the smile that said she and Chloe had talked about this earlier, without M in the room, and they'd agreed she could go too, but they wouldn't tell M, it would just happen. Then she gave the same smile to Chloe.

"Oh you can't go sweetie, you're too young. Another time, when Mummy and Daddy go too", she told Chloe.

The relief M felt was overwhelming, "Phew", the thought. With that Chloe stormed out of the kitchen again. This time Mum didn't follow her.

M moved his chair back and stood up. "Just going to the toilet", he said.

"You only went five minutes ago. Have you got a tummy ache?", Mum asked in a concerned way.

"I'm fine", said M, shaking his head, remembering the "Are these two cartons for me" question earlier. As he passed his picnic bag, he noticed a folded piece of paper tucked into one of the mesh pockets. He took it out, unfolded it and saw it was a note from Dad. It read, 'Have a great day. Be good for Mrs. Cross. Tell me all about it later. Love you, Dad xxx". This made M really excited, then he remembered what he needed to do. He dropped the paper onto the table and made his way to the downstairs loo before he had an accident. M hadn't wet his pants since he was five, and he wasn't about to do it again now.

At nine twenty five M was sat on the stairs, ready to go. Walking boots on, picnic bag ready and unable to keep still with excitement. He also had wellies in a supermarket bag for life, just in case. He couldn't find them in the garage earlier because Mum had already got them out.

At nine twenty seven, the fidgeting had got worse. M stood up, then sat down. He stood up, walked to the window, back to the stairs and sat down. He stood up, checked his picnic was still in the bag with the two cartons. Of course they were still there. It wasn't like a picnic could have grown legs and climbed out of the bag and invited the cartons to join them in an adventure all of their own back to the kitchen. He sat down on the stairs again.

At nine twenty nine M heard a car engine. Quickly he stood up, got his bags and walked to the window to check. Then came one of M's famous big sighs and a dejected look. The noise had been Mrs. Spooner's dog trainer turning up.

"Is that Mrs. Cross?", shouted Mum from the kitchen.

M tried to think of an answer that he could give that would make Mum think he'd misheard her, like she does to him. He tried to think what rhymes with 'Cross', but he actually couldn't think of anything at the moment, as he was too anxious about Mrs. Cross being late.

"No!", replied M emphatically, "It's Mrs. Spooner's dog person. Do you think she's forgotten?"

"Do I think Mrs. Spooner's dog's person's forgotten what?" asked Mum.

M frowned, "No, do you think Mrs. Cross has forgott....". He was mid-sentence when he saw Mrs. Cross' car turn the corner into his road.

"Bye Mum", he shouted and made for the door and opened it. The excitement was too much, and he had to drop the bags and run back into the house, leaving the front door wide open. He passed his Mum as she was coming from the kitchen.

"No walking boots on the carpet!!", she scolded.

"Sorry", said M not stopping, "Need a wee!", and carried on regardless.

As M got back from the loo, Mum had already transferred his booster seat into Mrs. Cross' car, and his bags were in her boot. They were all ready for the off. A day at the zoo, just what M had been waiting for.

Mrs. Cross made sure M was strapped in and he was comfortable, and with M confirming both were fine, she put the car in gear, and they set off, waving to Mum and Chloe as they left.

Mrs. Cross looked in her mirror every time she spoke to M. He had no idea why she did this. It was as if she was waiting to 'see' the words coming out of M's mouth when he spoke. M's mind went into a bit of overdrive. If she could see the words coming out of his mouth, because she was seeing them in the mirror, they'd be the wrong way around, so she couldn't have read them anyway, unless she could read backwards.

"Are you looking forward to today?".

M just nodded. Although he knew Mrs. Cross, and although Mrs. Cross was a friend of him Mum's, he hadn't actually been in her car with her on his own. He felt a little shy, and didn't really know what to say, which made him feel a little awkward.

"Mum says she's made you sandwiches". M nodded again, then plucked up the courage to speak.

"Cheese, ham and onion", he said, a little louder than he have liked, but it was too late to take it back, turn the volume down and say it again quieter.

"Yummy", said Mrs. Cross, "Well I've got plenty of picnic stuff if you get hungry".

M wondered what Mrs. Cross might have plenty of in her picnic bag, then all of a sudden, without warning his mouth started working without asking his brains permission.

"Where's your lollipop?". Oh how he wished he hadn't asked that question.

Mrs. Cross laughed, "Oh I don't take it everywhere I go, just to the crossing in the morning and the afternoon".

"Sorry", said M.

"Don't be sorry. I never think about it, and you're not the first child to ask or to think that I take it everywhere with me", she said smiling.

At the next traffic lights M got all excited because he saw the brown 'zoo' arrow sign pointing left. That meant they weren't far away. It was the sign that Chloe always pointed out. The sign meant they had to go left at these lights, then turn right a little way down that road and the zoo entrance was on the left of that road.

The lights changed to green and Mrs. Cross moved off and straight on. M looked through the window as they crossed over the crossroads and stared down the road, he thought they should be going.

"Dad always goes that way", he said as politely as he could and trying not to sound worried.

Mrs. Cross looked in the mirror at M.

"Don't worry, we're going in the back entrance", she said reassuringly.

"Oh"

"Well I figured that if the zoo was closed, there would be nobody at the entrance or on the gates, or at the turnstiles".

M nodded.

"So we'll go in the back entrance. It's ok, it's how I get in when I go and see Rob, I mean Mr. Stenson, if I'm visiting him", she said, noticing M looking anxious.

Sure enough, over another set of lights and a left turn they came to the rear entrance of the zoo. It wasn't as grand and fancy as the front, but why would it be? There were different signs to look at and read. At the front there were pictures of animals with speech bubbles; things like a crocodile saying, 'Hope you've brought your camera – Snap Snap!!' and a camel saying, 'There are humps in the road, please drive slowly'. At the back the signs read, 'Deliveries only' and 'Caution, please drive slowly 5mph max'. Pretty boring signs really M thought to himself.

There was a short drive from the road to some big green wooden gates. Mrs. Cross drove slowly towards the gates and stopped next to a post with a metal box on it. It looked like the intercom at the flats where his Grandma lived. There was a camera on this one that stared into the driver's window. Mrs. Cross lowered her window, looked into the camera and smiled, like she was going to have her photo taken.

"Hi, it's Jo", she said. She sort of shouted as if she didn't think her normal voice would have reached the intercom.

Nothing happened.

"That's funny", she said into the intercom, but talking to herself.

"Hello, it's Jo. Is Rob there?", she shouted a bit louder.

Still nothing happened. M didn't know what was supposed to happen, he just noticed that nothing happened. That and the fact that Mrs. Cross has said 'That's funny' made M sure that something was supposed to happen.

"Are you supposed to press the button?" asked M as helpfully as he could.

"Not normally, but I'll give it a go" she said opening her door. Mrs. Cross lifted her right leg out of the car and no sooner had she put her foot on the ground there was a crackling sound coming from the intercom.

With a smile into the camera and a little laugh, Mrs. Cross repeated, "Hi, it's Jo".

The crackling continued, like someone was talking but it wasn't getting all the way from where the person was speaking from to the intercom without getting garbled.

"Jo Cross, I've come to see Rob Stenson", said Mrs. Cross in a very business-like manner.

M thought that it sounded like aliens had taken over the intercom and were trying to communicate the best way they could but could only crackle.

"What's supposed to happen?", asked M inquisitively from the back.

Mrs. Cross now had both feet out of the car and was leaning towards the intercom stand and was pressing the button. As she pressed it the crackling stopped.

"Hi, it's Jo Cross", she said craning her neck to get her mouth as close to the speaker but keeping her body as close to the car as she could. She let go of the button – Crackling.

"The gate should open", she said and pressed again – Crackling stopped. Then she pressed the button a number of times, three or four times, as though she thought the button was broken. Crackling – Silence – Crackling – Silence – Crackling – Silence. Still nothing happened.

"Maybe nobody's home". M shouted this as Mrs. Cross was now fully out of the car and he was sure she wouldn't have heard his normal talking voice.

"Hmmmm", came the reply, like she'd heard him, but didn't agree.

"Should we go?". M was concerned, but also a little disappointed that he had to ask.

Mrs. Cross edged back into the car, and looked at M, in quite a serious way M thought.

"I'm going up to the gate, do you want to come or stay in the car?"

"I'll come", M replied nervously, although this may have been a time when his mouth worked without his brain's permission again. But he was sure he wanted to go. With that, Mrs. Cross lifted the seat lever which moved the back of her seat forward, so it was touching the steering wheel. In his Dad's car he had his own door, but in Mrs. Cross, he had to stand up being careful not to bang his head. He manoeuvred himself into the foot well, then very clumsily over the back of the driver's seat. He couldn't just jump out, like he did from Dad's, but had to get one leg out, making sure the leg he'd left in the car didn't get trapped under the driver's seat. He sort of made it with a little stumble.

"It's easier getting in than getting out", he said chuckling nervously.

Mrs. Cross took his hand, and they both walked towards the big green gates. They were solid, so you couldn't see through them, and they were arched so they were taller at the middle. M wondered why there was so much space between the intercom and the gates. He couldn't answer his own question and he didn't ask. There just was. As they got closer, the gates got bigger and he wondered why they were so tall. In M's mind and to M the gates were huge. Then the answer popped into his head. So a giraffe can't see over the top. Of course! As they got nearer, M could only see green wood, nothing else. He looked up expecting not to be able to see the top of the gates any longer because they'd be in the clouds. But they weren't. He could see the top, and as his gaze lowered, he saw where Mrs. Cross was heading for. Within the gates on the right hand side was a smaller gate. It was closed, but to the right of it was another intercom, this one didn't have a camera, and a label underneath the button read, 'Press for assistance'.

Without any hesitation, Mrs. Cross pressed the button.

M didn't know if he was nervous or excited. It might have been both.

"Hi, it's Jo Cross. Can you open the gate please?", she said bending slightly to get mouth as close to the intercom as she could without actually kissing it.

Nothing again. No answer, no crackling, no open gate.

Mrs. Cross sighed, so M sighed too.

"Don't worry", she said to him, trying to reassure M and herself.

"Plan A" she continued, "Was to come in the back way and use the intercom to have the gates opened. Plan B was to press for assistance and have this gate opened. Time for plan C"

"What's plan C?", asked M, expecting a rather detailed answer, thinking that this had happened before and Mrs. Cross knew exactly what to do.

"No idea yet", came her rather undetailed reply, "But this is turning out to be rather trickier that I thought". She sounded quite upbeat and excited.

M thought that two gates not being opened, and two intercoms not working and not being able to get in the zoo was anything but exciting. Exciting would be to....

"Are we going to climb over the gates?", again mouth working, brain not in gear!

Mrs. Cross laughed out loud, just as she'd pressed the button to speak again. He'd never really heard Mrs. Cross laugh, but it was a loud and very hearty laugh. Her laugh reminded him of a witch's cackle, but he made sure his mouth stayed closed, as to tell her would have been really rude. As she released the button, they heard the crackle again followed by the same sort of laugh back at them through the intercom.

Mrs. Cross looked at M. M looked at Mrs. Cross, then they both looked at the now silent intercom.

"Someone's in there", Mrs. Cross said puzzled, "So why wouldn't they open the gates?"

M didn't answer because he thought Mrs. Cross was talking to herself, not to him.

Mrs. Cross pressed the intercom again and the sound of a horn blasted at the same time startling them both. In fact M felt as though he'd jumped out of his skin so much that he might struggle getting back into it. It was Mrs. Cross who turned to see a large delivery van parked behind her car waiting to come into the zoo.

The driver of the van was waving to them and pointing to Mrs. Cross' car. It was a red van, quite old, but clean. It had once had lettering on the side, but these had been peeled off, although you could see where the letters had been where the paint around them had faded. You could still make out the words G. M. Stanley & Sons. It also had a ladder up the left hand back door, and like a square roof rack which to M looked like an old bed frame on top. If it had cushions or padding around the sides, you could sit up there, M thought. Then he quickly thought about bridges and immediately dismissed the idea.

"That's it!", exclaimed Mrs. Cross, "Back in the car M. We'll follow that van".

Now this, thought M, was exciting. Following a delivery van into the zoo, and Mrs. Cross' words echoed in his head. "Follow that van", it was almost like a police chase. They made their way back to the car and climbed in. Mrs. Cross manoeuvred the car into a position so the van could pass, then she tucked her car behind the van.

The driver pulled forward slightly, then climbed out of his cab to use the intercom.

"Are you going to tell him it's not working?", M asked.

"Not yet, we'll wait and see what happens".

They waited for what seemed like five minutes, although it probably wasn't. Sure enough, nothing was happening. The driver came to the car. Mrs. Cross looked up from the driver's seat, and the driver bent down to her window.

"No answer", said the driver.

"No", said Mrs. Cross, at which the driver just shrugged his shoulders.

"We've heard a laugh", said M from the back seat, and the driver just shrugged again.

"Something's not right", Mrs. Cross told the driver, "My name's Jo Cross and this is M" she said looking into the back of the car. "We're trying to get in too. That intercom seems to be broken"

"And we heard a laugh through the other one", added M, pointing to the far intercom on the small gate.

"Funny that, I got in yesterday no problem", the driver told them, "Had to come back today to bring the rest of the animal feeds".

"So, they are expecting you?", inquired Mrs. Cross.

The driver had returned to the intercom and was pressing the button. He looked back at the car.

"Crackling", he shouted.

"Just told you that", said Mrs. Cross under her breath.

M smiled at this, but then his brain went into gear and his eyes looked up towards the back of the van. He had an idea. Mrs. Cross wasn't going to like it and he needed the driver to move his van, and he needed to get out of the car.

"Can I go and try the small gate again?", he asked, hopefully.

"I don't see why not", replied Mrs. Cross, and she let M out of the car. He'd learned from last time that he needed to get the right foot out of the car first, followed by the wrong foot. If he got the wrong foot out first his right foot would get trapped and he'd stumble. Once out he walked towards the driver who was still pressing the intercom.

"I'm going to try the small gate again", he said as he passed the driver, "Why don't you drive down to the gate?"

Again the driver just shrugged, but M didn't see this as he now had his back to the driver. Even though he'd shrugged he must have thought it was a good idea as he left the intercom, returned to his van and started the engine. By the time he'd edged up to the gate M was at the intercom already. As the driver had moved his van forward, so Mrs. Cross had moved her car and pulled up right behind the van. She was certain that anyone opening the gate would see the van, but not her car.

The driver got out and joined M.

"Heard a laugh through this one", M told the driver. He was expecting another shrug of the driver's shoulders.

"What kind of laugh?", asked the driver, surprising M. His voice was quite gentle and not the sort of voice M had expected. The driver was a big man, wearing a tee-shirt that was at least a size too small for him and very worn jeans. His big black boots were dirty. M didn't know what they were dirty with, and it didn't really matter. M was thinking of other things, like distraction tactics.

M wanted to say, "A laugh like Mrs. Cross", but if you hadn't heard Mrs. Cross laugh you wouldn't know what that was like, so couldn't imagine what the intercom laugh was like, so he didn't bother.

"More of a cackle really", said M. With that the driver pressed the intercom button.

When he spoke into the intercom his voice changed to a more gruffly sounding voice. Maybe because he was bending, maybe because he was getting frustrated at not being let in like he had yesterday.

Mrs. Cross now joined M and the driver at the intercom. Whoever was at the other end couldn't see there was now three people trying to get into the zoo.

"Was everything ok yesterday?" asked Mrs Cross.

"Don't know. Just dropped and left", replied the driver.

"You didn't speak to anyone?"

"Nah... The main gate opened, I drove in, dropped and drove out".

"Oh". Mrs Cross was a bit non-plussed by this.

The driver and Mrs. Cross were chatting now, and it was M's chance to spring into action. He pretended to be trying to look through imaginary gaps in the big solid gate. When he was sure the other two were concentrating on the intercom and deep in conversation, he quickly sneaked to the back of the van.

CHAPTER FOUR: INTO THE ZOO AND BEYOND

Once around the back of the van, he checked the ladder on the back by trying to pull it off the door. It didn't move an inch and the door didn't open. What's more, his pulling on the ladder didn't make a noise. He hoisted himself up onto the first rung and made sure he was steady. Carefully he climbed, making sure he had both feet on the rung before he climbed onto the next. Eventually his head and chest were above the roof of the van. He look down behind him. He wasn't that high, but it felt high. M couldn't remember ever being this high off the ground. He must have been. Surely the climbing frame in the park him Mum took him too was higher than this?

Now the tricky part. He had to clamber over the top of the roof rack so he could get inside it and onto the roof. He could see that the base frame on the top of the van was made up of a metal grid, so when he was over, he wouldn't be directly on the van's roof. As light as he was, he didn't want to make dints in the roof where he stepped. M got both arms over the top of the railing and his feet onto the last rung of the ladder. One leg over, then the other, but he slipped a little and fell into the roof rack. Luckily, he didn't make a sound. He'd only fell about four inches, which just made him go "oofph" very quietly. He composed himself and made his way slowly along the grid to the front of the van, on the passenger side, making sure that the driver and Mrs. Cross didn't see him. He could still hear them discussing the dilemma they were all in but couldn't hear the exact words.

Once at the front M was able to stand up. If he looked to his right, he could see the driver and Mrs. Cross still at the intercom. If he looked behind him the van seemed to be longer than he remembered walking along, and he could just see the end of Mrs. Cross' car roof. His legs wobbled a bit, just like they did at the top of the climbing frame. He crouched to steady himself, and after a few seconds stood up again. This time he looked straight on and over the gates. He could see the roof of a building but nothing else as he was a bit too far away from the gates. He was certain though, if the van was nearer, he would have a clear view into the back of the zoo. It was at that moment he heard the driver's exact words.

"Right, well I better be off", he told Mrs. Cross.

M panicked slightly. If the driver moved, no, he didn't even want to think about it. He had to act fast and act brave. His Mum would have told him he was stupid, his Dad would have shouted, "Get down from there now", and Chloe would have just laughed and ask if she could go up too.

Brain in gear, he moved over to the driver's side and asked calmly, "Can you move your van a little closer to the gate please?"

He couldn't help but laugh out loud when he saw both Mrs. Cross and the driver look around for M. Then they realised that the voice was coming from above them, and they both turned to face the van and look up. There was M standing tall on the top of the van looking very pleased with himself.

"Oh my!", exclaimed Mrs. Cross.

"What the?", was all the driver could say.

"M come down this minute", said Mrs. Cross almost scolding as his Mum would have done.

"If you get the van closer to the gate, I can see right over it. It's quite safe", said M, trying to reassure both the driver and in particular Mrs. Cross. "In fact the climbing frame at the park is higher than this", M carried on.

"Please come down M", pleaded Mrs. Cross.

The driver opened his cab door to get in.

"What are you doing?". Mrs. Cross had shouted this, and as she did, they all heard the laugh again diverting any attention that was on M back to the intercom.

"Sit down and hold on", shouted the driver from the cab.

"No!!", shouted Mrs. Cross, "It's too dangerous".

"I'll be fine", shouted M back settling himself into the cage like frame on the roof and feeling like Indiana Jones.

"Just be careful", Mrs. Cross shouted, "I hope your Mum doesn't find out about this".

"Are you sat down?", shouted the driver.

"Yes", shouted M and Mrs. Cross together, although Mrs. Cross' yes was a little more anxious than M's.

"Don't move until I tell you to".

M assumed he was talking to him and not Mrs. Cross.

The driver looked at the back of the van, and asked Mrs. Cross to move her car a little, which she did. The driver reversed about a metre, then forward turning right. He stopped short of the kerb, then reversed again, moving the van towards the gate, making sure that he did so smoothly and carefully so as not to jolt or frighten M on top. Despite feeling like Indiana Jones, both hands gripped the top rail of the cage so tightly that his knuckles were white. The van stopped, then edged forward, just as smoothly, then stopped again. The driver had actually parked the van side on to the gate. The engine stopped, but M didn't move because nobody had told him he could.

"I figured if I just moved forward the bonnet would be in the way. Side on the van is a lot closer to the gate", he told Mrs. Cross, looking at his watch. "I need to call my boss; I'm going to be late for my next drop".

"Good idea", came the reply.

"I'll call them now, before this gets any more complicated".

The driver got out his phone and started to dial. Meanwhile, M was still sat sitting motionless until he heard the driver, Mrs. Cross or anyone tell him he could move. He could see the road that lead up to the back gate of the zoo right up to where it meets the main road. Well he could almost see the main road. There were a couple of trees in the way. Every now and then he could hear the faint sound of a car going past, then he'd see the wheels. In between the cars he would hear larger vehicles, lorries, which he could just see the tops of. If he looked slightly left, he could see the tops of the lorry cabs as they passed behind a wall, then the sides with whatever the lorries had written on them. His eyes followed a Tesco lorry from left to right, and he wondered if it was lunch time yet. Probably not was his second thought.

Any thought of lunch was dismissed as his eyes met with the far right hand side of the van he was on and Mrs. Cross' head peeping over the top railing as she climbed the ladder. She looked scared. She looked even more scared than M felt. In fact if at this moment they had a 'who is more scared contest', Mrs Cross would win by a country mile, as his Dad would say.

"It's quite safe", M told her as Mrs. Cross struggled to get herself off the ladder and onto the roof of the van.

"Right", shouted the driver looking around for Mrs. Cross, then looked up at M and saw him and Mrs. Cross on top of the van.

"Oh", he carried on, "There's a party on the roof there?" He noticed M still sat in the corner looking at him.

"Can I move yet?", M asked.

"Oh sure, all secure", he told M, then looked at Mrs. Cross, "I've told them I've got a puncture and having difficulty getting the wheel off. They were going to send a relief van, but I put them off. I've only got one delivery after this, then it's back to the depot".

M wondered if the driver would tell the others back at the depot about his adventure.

Mrs. Cross just nodded as she was afraid to talk in case it took away any of the concentration she was using to get across the top of the van.

M immediately stood up and turned to face the gates of the zoo. The gates were still waist height to him, but he had a clear view of the animal feed building. The windows were tinted to keep the sun out so keeping the inside of the building cool. M couldn't see through the tint that well, but he thought he could see movement. He looked behind him and Mrs. Cross was almost next to him. As she crouched alongside him, she breathed a huge sigh of relief.

"If you look in the corner window over there", he pointed left, "Can you see someone in there?"

"Possibly", Mrs. Cross replied, "Or it could be", she trailed off and craned her neck slightly to get a better view of the road that ran along the back of the building. "No, I thought it could have been a reflection of someone walking along the road, but it can't be".

The driver had now joined them on top of the van.

"I think it's Mr. Stenson, I think I can see his hat", M told the pair of adults now crouched on his left hand side.

"If it is, there's someone with him", added Mrs. Cross. She looked at the driver.

M squinted a little, hoping that it would give him a better view. If he'd have known he would be stood on top of a van, he's have packed his binoculars. They weren't real binoculars. They'd come in a bird watching set his Grandma had given him last Christmas with a book on garden birds.

"There's definitely movement in there", Mrs. Cross told them, "But I can't make out who –", she stopped talking and squinted like M. "Is it Charlie?"

"Who's Charlie?" asked the driver. "I know Paul who checked deliveries off sometimes. He makes an awful cup of tea".

"Charlie's the chimp", M told him. "He's quite tame". "He was brought to the zoo as a baby about four years ago, a rescue chimpanzee".

"He only comes out of his enclosure when there's nobody about", explained Mrs. Cross, "Like when the zoo is open, he's not allowed out. Only when the zoo is closed".

As they all squinted, they all saw what they thought was Charlie jump onto what they thought was a table next to who they thought was Mr. Stenson.

"It is Charlie!", shouted M.

"Have you met this Charlie?", the driver asked, quite startled at M's exclamation.

"You probably have the number of times you've been here", interrupted Mrs. Cross.

"Three times", confirmed M, "I held his hand the last time, "Mr. Stenson said Charlie only held hands with people he trusted", he boasted.

In the building they were looking at sure enough, Mr. Stenson and Charlie were preparing fruit and seeds for the parrots in the aviary. As quickly as Mr. Stenson was preparing it, Charlie was throwing it into a bucket. Every now and then the chopped fruit wouldn't make the bucket. It didn't even make it into the air, instead it made its way straight into Charlies mouth. Mr. Stenson just smiled, and conceded that this was Charlie helping, as only Charlie knew how.

Every now and then, when he wasn't chopping, Mr. Stenson would look out of the window that faced the gates. He looked at the clouds moving across the sky, assessing if it was windy or not and if it was going to rain. His gaze would follow a bird flying from left to right, and from right to left, or from the roof of the building to the bird feeder that stood under a cherry tree across the zoo perimeter road.

It was as he followed a pigeon from right to left that his eyes met the big green gates. He stopped following the bird, and his eyes focused at the top of the gates. Was that a head he saw? No, couldn't have been, and he ignored the thought. Then he ignored the ignoring of the thought and decided to go and investigate.

On the top of the van;

"All get down", whispered Mrs. Cross

All three ducked down behind the top of the gates. They were all sure Mr. Stenson had looked directly at them.

"What do you call a one eyed dinosaur", asked the driver.

"Dunno", said M. looking at the driver, a little white after having to hide so quickly and being filled with adrenalin.

"A Doyouthinkhesaurus".

M just stared blankly at him, no laugh, no smile, no smirk. The driver however was chuckling to himself, as this joke had clearly tickled him.

"A Do-u-think-he-saw-us", the driver said, attempting to explain the joke.

"I get it", said M, "I just don't think it's funny"

The driver went back to just shrugging, as he did when they first met.

"This is no time for silliness", scolded Mrs. Cross, and made the first move to peer over the gates again. M stood up slowly and joined her in the peering. The Driver decided now was a good time to check his phone for updates from his office.

Actually, now was not a good time as both M and Mrs. Cross were greeted with Mr. Stenson and Charlie, walking towards the gates, slowly, but purposefully. He'd obviously seen them and wanted to know what they were doing, not only outside the gates, but peering over them like naughty school kids. Well there was one school kid, although it was end of term, so officially he was a holiday kid as school was closed!

Mrs. Cross decided to take matters into her own hands.

"Hi Rob, It's Jo. Can we come in?", she shouted from the roof of the van and over the gate.

"Hi Mr. Stenson", shouted M. On the back of Mrs. Cross shouting, he plucked up the courage to do the same.

Mr. Stenson continued his walk to the gates, his gaze firmly fixed to the upper part of them, flitting from Mrs. Cross to M, and back to Mrs. Cross again.

Mrs. Cross frowned as if puzzled by something. She didn't want to let M know anything of her thoughts, so she changed her frown to a smile.

"He has no idea who we are", she thought to herself, and smiled at M.

M Looked at Mrs. Cross and smiled back, then thought to himself, "He's forgotten who I am". M tried to remember the last time he came to the zoo. It can't have been so long ago that Mr. Stenson had forgotten all about him. When he went away on summer holidays, he wouldn't come to the zoo for four of five weeks. When he did visit again, Mr. Stenson always remembered him. Why not now?

"Rob, it's me – Jo Cross", she said again, trying to at least jog his memory. She knew it had been a while since she'd been to see him, but even if she hadn't been for six months, whenever she'd returned, she'd always had a warm welcome and a hug. So why not now??

The driver, who decided in his own mind that he couldn't remember ever meeting the Stenson fella, knelt up and looked over the gates.

"I've got a delivery for you, should have been here yesterday with the other stuff, but delivering it today", said the driver, not even bothering to introduce himself.

Mr. Stenson looked right at the driver, he seemed to acknowledge that he'd spoken. It was then that the strangest thing Mrs. Cross, M and the driver had ever seen happened. They just stared unable to speak. They wanted to speak, but no works would come out of either of their mouths. The driver stared, eyes like saucers, and his mouth fell open as if he'd heard a dentist in his head say, "Open wide".

Mr. Stenson chattered and screeched like a chimpanzee would, flailing his arms above his head, whilst shaking his head and baring his teeth. Then he cackled. The same cackle that M had heard through the second intercom.

Charlie the chimpanzee also looked up at the driver, like a chimpanzee would, then looked at Mr. Stenson chattering and flailing.

"Well done on getting it here this morning", said the chimp, "We've just used our last and were hoping there wouldn't be a long delay".

M looked at Mrs. Cross, Mrs. Cross looked at M, they both looked at the driver, then they all stared back at Mr. Stenson in complete disbelief in what had just taken place.

With that Charlie smiled a chimp like smile and turned his head to face Mr. Stenson, who in turn was studying Mrs. Cross' face above the gate, moving his head from side to side, like a dog would do if you showed it a really clever card trick.

Again, Mr. Stenson chattered and flailed, and this time jumped up and down on the spot, the simply turned his back on them all.

Again, the chimp stood upright, looked at Mrs. Cross, who smiled. The chimp then turned his attention to M, who also smiled, and then the chimp announced;

"I'm sorry, who did you say you were? We don't recall having appointments with yourselves today. Do you have appointments?"

The chimp then sat down, as chimps do, and started to pick his own toenails.

Mrs. Cross was dumbfounded, as was M. It was the driver that noticed M's eyes all teary and ready to overflow. He put his hand on M's shoulder and squeezed lightly as a delivery driver's way of saying 'there, there, chip up'.

"Look", he said to M, "I have absolutely no idea what is going on here, and I have doubly absolutely no idea what I just saw". He squeezed M's shoulder again, "I know it looked all wrong, which probably means it needs to be put right".

"He didn't know who I was", M replied, "He always knows who I am", he continued, "Why doesn't he know me?"

Mrs. Cross overheard and joined them on M's side of the van roof, "If it's any consolation M, he didn't know me either, and as upsetting as it is, we have to find out why he doesn't know us anymore"

The driver was looking at Mrs. Cross and M as she was talking, first one, then the other, his face frowning and getting frownier and frownier.

"Excuse me", the driver interjected, "I understand perfectly that Rob or Mr. Stenson doesn't know either of you, or claims not to know you anymore, but... Did anybody see a talking chimp just then, or was that just me?"

"I was coming to that", replied Mrs. Cross

"Oh thank goodness for that!", the relieved driver said with a hefty sigh.

"Something is very wrong here, and as we seem to be the only people to know about it, only we can help", Mrs. Cross said to both M and the driver.

"We?", queried the driver, "Who is we? I'm just a delivery guy, here to deliver. I am not we!"

"You saw what just happened", Mrs. Cross responded.

"I know what I saw, and I know what I heard. And I know I've got a delivery to make and a pretend puncture to fix".

"Exactly!", Mrs Cross retorted, "If only we know, only we can find out what's happened here. We can't tell anyone".

"Why not?" asked the driver.

"What are you going to say? Who would believe you?"

The driver thought for a second. He didn't believe what he'd just witnessed, so how could he explain it to anyone else?

Mrs. Cross interrupted his thoughts, "You saw the zoo owner acting like a monkey, heard him speak like a monkey, and then a chimpanzee translate into the Queen's English?"

It did sound a bit farfetched. The driver shook his head. She was right, who would believe him. He didn't believe it himself, even though he's just witnessed it. He looked at M, and then back at Mrs. Cross. M was still sat looking very teary, not because Mr. Stenson acted like a chimp and not because the chimp had spoken. He was still upset that he didn't remember him.

"We have to find a way into the zoo and get to the bottom of this", Mrs. Cross said, very seriously. "Something isn't right, we know it isn't right and...". She was interrupted by a short burst of music, then a female voice singing 'Shake It Off'. M recognised it as part of a pop song but couldn't remember who's the voice was. As the 'Shake It Off' repeated, Mrs. Cross took her phone out of her pocket.

"It's your Mum", she said to M, "Texting to see if we're having a good day".

"What are you going to tell her?", M wondered out loud.

"Yeah, what are you going to tell her", repeated the driver.

"To be honest, if I told her we couldn't get into the zoo, that we were sitting on top of a van and we'd just been spoken to by a chimp, she'd actually smile. She'd probably think I was making it up and that M and me were having a great zoo adventure".

The driver shrugged. "If I told my boss that, he'd probably tell me to take some time off, make me an appointment at the doctors, and suggest they take my driving licence off me".

Mrs. Cross started to reply to M's Mum's text.

"What are you going to tell her?" asked M.

"I'll just say we're having an unexpectedly bizarre day", Mrs. Cross told him. "I won't lie, but I won't tell her the truth".

"Send", she said out loud as she pressed the send button.

Within in seconds 'Shake It Off' sounded again.

"She's says 'good'", Mrs. Cross told them.

M smiled.

"Taylor Swift? Seriously? As a text alert?", asked the driver.

Mrs. Cross just smiled.

"That's it!", exclaimed M.

Both Mrs. Cross and the driver looked at M.

"I couldn't remember who's that voice was. It's Taylor Swift", M told them.

"Oh", the driver said dejectedly, "I thought you had a plan then"

"Nobody at school would believe me either", M announced.

"What? That someone you know has Taylor Swift telling them they have a text?" joked the driver.

"He means about this", laughed Mrs. Cross pointing to the green gates.

"Wait!" said M suddenly, "What if", he stopped himself to think it through, then continued,

"What if we hid in the back of your van. They would let you in and we could jump out when you made the delivery".

The driver laughed a silent laugh, and Mrs. Cross just smiled a consoling smile and then looked at each other, both silently agreeing it was a mad idea.

"It could work", M said trying to convince them both.

"Actually, I'm not allowed to take passengers in the back. I could get the sack".

"Just through the gates", added M.

Mrs. Cross looked at M, the 'mad idea smile' she'd given the driver had now turned into a 'you may have an idea' smile directed at M.

"Yes, just through the gates. M, you're a genius", she told M.

"You're not serious?", the driver asked them, looking at each of them in turn.

Mrs. Cross' mind was now working overtime to formulate an instant plan to get her and M into the zoo using the van.

"Like a Trojan Horse", exclaimed M, rather excited that he's remembered something off a history website his Dad had shown him.

"Brilliant", exclaimed Mrs. Cross just as excited, "We'll pretend we've gone away, but get in your van. You ask

Mr. Stenson, Rob, if you can go in to make the delivery. You distract him and Charlie".

"Charlie?" asked the driver.

"The chimpanzee", M clarified.

"Then we'll climb out of the van and... Well I don't know what we'll do until we get in there", added Mrs. Cross.

"No. No. No no no no no", is all the driver could say.

"Oh please", pleaded M, who was by now so excited by the plan, he's almost forgotten that he was upset at not being remembered by Mrs Stenson.

"Please errm? We don't even know your name", remarked Mrs. Cross

The driver had gone back to shrugging.

"I don't know", the driver said unsurely.

"You don't know what your name is", smiled M, thinking that would be something his Dad would say.

"I don't know about you two getting in the back and me driving you in. And my name is Stu, not that it matters".

"It matters", replied Mrs. Cross, "Because now we can say please Stu!"

"Tell you what", suggested Stu, "I'll take you in, but once you're in I'm having nothing to do with it and I'll be leaving and be on my way,".

"Perfect", agreed Mrs. Cross. "M come with me, whilst Stu gets the gate open".

Both Mrs. Cross and M scuttled away across the van roof away from the gates, then towards the ladder. Stu stood up to look over the gates and addressed Mr. Stenson, who was still stood just outside the zoo feed building. The chimp was nowhere to be seen, although Stu had a feeling it wouldn't be far away.

Stu coughed to get Mr. Stenson's attention, who promptly turned to face the gates and looked up. Stu smiled at him, and Mr. Stenson smiled back with a much wider grin showing more teeth than Stu thought was possible when smiling.

"If you can let me in, I can drop this delivery off", Stu said nervously, not knowing if Mr. Stenson would understand him.

With a flail of the hands and arms and three monkey-like jumps on the spot, Mr. Stenson then walked towards the gate quite normally.

Quickly, Stu went to the ladder, scrambled down and ran to the cab door and got in. He started the engine assuming that M and Mrs. Cross were in the back already and had added a bit to their plan.

The gate opened, first the left hand side, then the right. They were electric, so Mr. Stenson must be behind the left hand gate pressing the button. As soon as the opening of the gates was wide enough, Stu drove the van through, slowly and steadily, into the zoo. Stu knew that once inside he had to distract anyone from seeing the other two getting out of the van. Stu looked into his side mirror. He could see Mr. Stenson, obviously pressing the close button, as the left hand gate looked as though it had stopped opening. It was actually at that point of changing direction. The chimp was also with him at the gate controls. Stu had no idea how it'd got there, but there it was.

Stu drove a little further, swung the van around and reversed up to the corner of the building on his left hand side. Quickly he got out and made his way, just as quickly to the back of the van. He opened the doors and like a couple of special commandoes Mrs. Cross and M scurried out, around the corner of the building and out of sight. No distraction needed on his part.

Stu grabbed the large cardboard box from the van. He wanted to have the box on the pavement and be back in his cab before he had to encounter the chimp at close range. The box was heavy and awkward to lift, but he managed to get it where he wanted. It was only three or four steps from van to pavement and a couple of huffs and puffs. He retraced the same few steps to the back of the van and closed the door.

As Stu closed the van door, there they were, stood there, looking menacing, although that was just in Stu's mind. They weren't menacing at all. They were just standing there waiting for the delivery.

Mr. Stenson Smiled, a huge wide smile.

"ooh ooh arrrrgh arrrrrgh chitter chitter chatter chatter", he shrieked, almost so loud it hurt Stu's ears.

"Ahem", the chimp started again clearing his throat, "Once again, many thanks for this", he said. The chimp then looked at Mr. Stenson as if looking for confirmation that the interpretation was correct. Mr. Stenson nodded, and the chimp nodded back.

Stu couldn't wait to get back in his van, but the man and chimp were blocking his path. He took a couple of steps backwards towards the pavement, then turned quickly to run around the other side of his van, around the front and into the driver's door. By the time he got there, Mr. Stenson and his friend were making their way back to the gate control. Stu started the engine, and as soon as there was room for his van to get through, he exited the zoo compound.

The gates mechanism meant that the gate had to fully open before it could close again. By the time it was fully open, Mr. Stenson and the chimp could see Mrs. Cross' car still parked where she'd left it before clambering onto the top of Stu's van. Mr. Stenson looked at the car. The chimp looked at Mr. Stenson, then they both looked around to see if they could see anyone that owned it lurking. They couldn't. Mrs. Cross and M could see both Mr. Stenson and the chimp studying the car from where they were hiding. As the gate began to close, Mr. Stenson and Charlie both turned and started back towards the building.

Mrs. Cross and M quickly ducked back behind the corner.

"I forgot about my car", she whispered to M.

"And my lunch", added M

"Are you hungry?"

"Not yet, too scared to be hungry", replied M.

"Me too!"

"We need to keep out of sight", Mrs. Cross told M.

Back at M's house, Mum was baking with Chloe in the cooking part and Dad was at the kitchen table working on his laptop.

"I wonder how M's getting on with Jo?", she asked. There was no answer. Chloe was fully immersed in cracking eggs into a large bowl. She hit the egg so hard on the side of the bowl some of the white went onto the work top instead of in the bowl.

"mmmmm", murmured Dad concentrating.

"Maybe he's been swallowed whole by a hippo", Mum suggested.

"mmmmm", murmured Dad again.

On hearing Mum's suggestion, Chloe lost concentration and whacked an egg on the side so hard it almost exploded.

"Oh, don't hit them so hard darling", Mum said to Chloe.

"I wasn't", insisted Dad, "But sometimes the L key sticks", he explained.

"I was talking to Chloe about the eggs. I was talking to you about M".

"What about M?", Dad asked looking puzzled.

"He's been eaten in a hole by a hipposotasaurus", Chloe replied.

Dad looked at Chloe, then at Mum.

"I knew you weren't listening", Mum told Dad, then to Chloe "One more egg Chloe then we can add the sugar"

They were making a cake. Chloe loved baking days with Mummy, but there was always so much mess. Chloe took another egg out of the box, then noted the mess she's made with the last one. She put the egg on the worktop, reached across Mum to get a cloth to wipe up. As she wiped, a little too vigorously, raw egg was smeared, and she caught the new egg with the cloth and sent it spinning off the worktop towards the table. It landed with a splat on the floor right next to Dad's chair.

"Well there's no need to throw eggs at me!" said a startled Dad.

Chloe's face was a picture of shock at the speed the egg flew, and a little worry as to what Mum might say.

"Serves you right for not listening", laughed Mum, "I said I wonder how M is getting on at the zoo".

"Oh he'll be fine", Dad replied, "He's with Jo".

Meanwhile, back at the zoo Mrs. Cross and M had made their way to the nearest toilets they could find. With all the excitement of getting into the zoo and hiding from Mr. Stenson and Charlie, they were both bursting. Both of them had to think about unnecessary noise, so had to abandon the usual habits, and agreed neither of them would flush. Mrs. Cross thought it best no to make any noise that may alert anyone of their presence. M agreed. With that he went into the ladies with Mrs. Cross so they wouldn't be separated. He pee'd in silence. He even did a sitting down one, so he didn't make a splashing noise in the toilet water. He didn't flush, which he didn't feel good about, but they'd agreed. He opened the cubicle as quietly as he could, washed his hands and was just about to use the hand dryer when he felt a hand on each shoulder pulling him away. He turned swiftly thinking it was Mr. Stenson or Charlie to see it was Mrs. Cross now with one finger of her right hand on her lips. That was international teacher sign language for silence, which he recognised instantly. The relief of seeing it was Mrs. Cross was immense.

M put his hand to his mouth, which was international kids sign language for 'OOPS!'.

Mrs. Cross smiled a smile that meant 'Oh that was close', and again she put a finger to her lips. She went to the door first and peered out to check that the coast was clear.

"We need to be careful", she whispered. "Mr. Stenson and Charlie could be anywhere".

What she actually hoped was that he and Charlie were back in the animal feeds room sorting out the animal's meals now that Stu had delivered the extra feed that should have been here yesterday.

"We need to stay together", she whispered further.

M just nodded confirming he understood, and with that Mrs. Cross identified a route she thought they should take.

"If we go around the back of the loos towards the men's, then take the short path to the café opposite".

M nodded, again confirming he understood. At the mere mention of the café, he remembered his lunch in the car, and wondered how on earth they were going to retrieve that.

"Is it lunchtime yet?", M whispered.

Mrs, Cross looked at her watch, "Not yet, and besides our lunches are in the car!"

M had a watch at home, but he couldn't wear it. It was a Spiderman watch, which was a Christmas present. It had a blue and red striped strap with a buckle on. Had, being the operative word. Chloe had decided that she wanted a sash to dress one of her dolls as an air hostess and decided to cut the strap of M's watch. Mum and Dad were very angry with her that day. So M's watch was hanging on a piece of ribbon next to his bed.

M knew exactly where his lunch was, and the more he thought about it, the more peckish be began to feel. Mrs. Cross could see the disappointment in his eyes.

"Are you hungry"

"A little", replied M in a whisper and nodding just in case Mrs. Cross couldn't hear him.

Mrs. Cross took another look outside by peeping out of the ladies toilet door.

"Stay with me, and follow my instructions", she whispered. She didn't whisper too sternly, but M knew she meant it, and the thought of sneaking around the zoo trying not to be seen made him both nervous and excited.

Mrs, Cross looked right, left and right again. The looking both ways applied to here as well as crossing the road with a lollipop. After she'd looked right for the second time, she motioned for M to follow her out of the ladies, around the back to the gent's and they tucked themselves into the doorway there.

"Why do men's toilets always smell?" she whispered to M.

M just shrugged. M knew men's toilets smelled, but he had no idea how Mrs. Cross knew. Surely, she didn't use the gent's toilets. Did she? M dismissed the thought as Mrs. Cross again motioned for him to follow her after another right, left, right check, and they both made their way to the café door in a walking run. Or was it a running walk?

The café door was a double door with a little porch around it. They both huddled in the corner as if sheltering from said rain. You could fit eight or nine people in the porch in the event of a surprise downpour. Mrs. Cross, ever vigilant, leant out looking right, left, right to make sure there was nobody about that would discover them. M looked out from his corner. He'd never seen the zoo so empty. Whenever he'd been to the zoo before, there were people everywhere, walking, standing, running, sitting. Now it was deserted, and it looked massive.

Mrs. Cross then waved her hand behind her back with her left hand, indicating to M to move to the opposite corner of the doorway. M didn't know what Mrs. Cross meant and stayed where he was. At first, he thought Mrs. Cross had farted and was wafting it away, but then she looked behind and pointed to the other corner. M was giggling silently, but then moved quickly to where he was supposed to go, and continued smiling at his first thought, and his mistake. Mrs. Cross didn't fart!!

As M moved slowly from one corner to the next, he thought Mrs. Cross had seen someone coming. He moved slowly, keeping his back to the doors to make sure he wasn't seen. As his back, and the slight weight, that was his, leaned against the other door he felt it give slightly. He thought it was just loose and the little give in the door was just the door moving against the bolts. He checked the door by pushing it with one hand. It opened a little. He took his hand off and it closed again. He tried again, a little harder this time, and sure enough the door opened a little more. He let go again and wondered if it would open all the way.

Mrs. Cross was still peering around the edges of the porch walls, looking for anyone that might see them, and more importantly planning their next move. Where to run to without being seen. What she'd like to do was run out of the porchway and around the back of the café to the other doorway. Neither of them had any way of knowing who was in the zoo, apart from Mr. Stenson and Charlie. If they were still in the animal feeds house, how long would it be before they started the feeding rounds? Which way would they go?

M turned around to face the doors and pushed gently. He felt the door give again, and with a little more pressure it did in fact open. He stuck his head in to listen for any signs of life. He was sure it was silent in the café, but couldn't be certain, so he slid in. Once in he let the door close gently so as not to make a noise. He was getting good at this not making a sound business. Even Mrs. Cross hadn't heard the door open or close. As the glass door shut, he could still see Mrs. Cross outside keeping watch.

Once inside, the café was eerily quiet. Usually is was bustling with activity. People queueing for food, sitting at tables, coming in and out, walking around with trays of food looking for empty tables. Today there was just M. He didn't have to queue or find an empty table; they were all empty except one at the far end that had drink bottles and cans on. There was other stuff there too but from this distance he couldn't tell what they were. M turned to face the doors again.

Mrs. Cross was sure there was nobody coming. She'd kept watch for all of five minutes and there was no sign of anyone coming or going, and it was safe for her and M to make a move.

"Are you ready M?", she whispered.

There was no answer.

Thinking that M had slipped into a daydream, she turned to tap M to tell him to get ready to run. Her gaze immediately went to the corner where she'd told M to go. No M!! Her heart skipped a beat that she'd lost him or that he'd gone missing. After a couple of seconds of her heart racing she could see her reflection in the glass of the door, and she thought she saw something move. She looked down at her front to see what on her was moving. Nothing. The door began to open inwards slowly, silently. Her heart was now in her mouth, and she was in danger of making a noise it was beating that loudly. M peered through the opening, smiling, looking very pleased with himself. Mrs. Cross' swallowed hard as if she was actually swallowing her heart back to where it should be. She was so relieved to see M stood on the other side of the door.

M opened the door fully almost inviting Mrs. Cross into the café. This time it was him with his finger on his lips to signal to Mrs. Cross not to make a noise. She entered, holding the door open for herself, then closing it carefully so it didn't either slam or close noisily. M pointed to the table with the bottles and cans on.

"Someone's been here", he whispered. Mrs. Cross looked in the direction of the table.

"I wonder if the other door is open", she replied pointing to the double doors on the far side of the café similar to those they'd just come through.

To the right of the door was a row of around seven large windows. Each had a mural of an animal enclosure on; Lions, Elephants, Penguins, Meercats, camels, and sealions. The middle window had a mural of the entrance to the zoo with the name of the zoo, Chalford Zoo. The murals weren't painted on but were like large window shaped stickers. M remembered that they were special stickers because you could see out if you were in, but you couldn't see in if you were out.

"Only one way to find out", said M walking towards them.

"Wait! We have to be as quiet in here as we do out there", Mrs. Cross told him.

CHAPTER FIVE: THE EMPTY CAFÉ

They made their way into the café. On their left was a fridge with labels indicating the sandwiches that should have been stacked on the empty shelves. Tuna Mayonnaise, Egg and Cress, Ham and tomato and a Children's lunchbox (Choose any four items for £1.99).

There was a stack of trays waiting to be taken by the designated person who was to queue for food, whilst the others reserved the table. They passed the trays treading carefully and silently, following the tray slide, past another display fridge where drinks would have been for sale. Past the hot food counter that was stone cold.

The last hot meal served was homemade meat and potato pie, chips and peas for £3.95. This was written on the specials board behind the hot counter, but streaky from where someone had wiped it with a damp cloth and smeared the chalk.

They came to the hot drink counter and the till. There was a display of wrapped cakes and chocolate bars but no-one to buy them. It was here that they could see the table more clearly. Mrs. Cross took two chocolate bars and two wrapped cakes from the display and put them in her pocket. M looked shocked at what Mrs. Cross had just done, a look which Mrs. Cross noticed.

"I'll pay for them", she insisted.

M looked at the till, and the fact that nobody was there to take her money or open the till, then back at Mrs. Cross.

"Well obviously not now", she said smiling.

They moved from the servery, around the till and into an alcove that would have housed two tray trolleys. People who had finished their food would put their trays of dirty crockery and cutlery into the trolley ready for someone to wheel it into the kitchen for washing. From here they could see the table M had pointed to.

Sure enough, there were bottles and cans on it as well as two empty plates full of crumbs. One had crusts of bread on, so whoever had used that plate didn't like them. There were also two white mugs. They couldn't see if there was any liquid in either and they didn't want to check in case someone walked past the window. M had a brainwave, that he believed Mrs. Cross had forgotten or didn't know. The windows and the pictures on them were special. M's Dad called them one way windows.

You could see out whilst having your lunch, but you couldn't see in if you were walking past.

M got down on his hands and knees and crawled quickly to the dirty table. Once there he stayed as low as he could, below table height, then slowly raised himself to rest his elbows on one of the chairs. The area around the servery the floor was tiled, but where the tables and chairs were situated it was carpeted. It was a rough carpet, not like his Mum and Dad had in their house, which were soft.

"What are you doing?" Mrs. Cross whispered loudly to M.

M ignored her; he was too engrossed in his own little mission to the dirty table.

"Someone might see you", Mrs. Cross whispered emphatically.

M raised himself a little higher so he could see the top of the table more clearly.

"It's yesterday's paper", M whispered back.

"Feel the cups"

M looked at Mrs. Cross slightly puzzled at the request but did as he was told and felt the cups.

"Are they warm?

"Cold"

"They've not been here for a while then"

M deduced, as did Mrs. Cross, that because it was yesterday's paper and the cups were cold, this was yesterday's lunch. This was verified by the fact that the bread crusts were rock hard.

Mrs. Cross crawled across the floor to join him. She picked up the newspaper. It was the local free paper, The Chalford Messenger. The headline on the front read, "Chalford Zoo Closed", and a report on the closure by local reporter Maddie Taylor. Mrs. Cross skip read the report to try and find if Maddie had any insight into why it was closed. As far as she could make out, the report was quite generalised. It told readers is was closed, how children and families would be disappointed this summer and how Mr. Stenson hadn't been available for comment.

Whilst Mrs. Cross was reading, M had moved towards the other double doors, and was crouched behind a carousel of leaflets stood in a corner highlighting other attractions in the area and some a little further away. He'd used his common sense and was stood in the corner, so the carousel was almost in front of him. There were farm parks, steam engines, museums, summer fetes and nature trails. M looked to the top of the carousel and thought how high it looked from a crouching position. Then his attention was moved to the doors as one opened, not fully, but about a door's width, just enough for M to be able to tell that it wasn't locked or on a catch. Nobody came in and nobody had gone out, and it made no noise as it closed to meet the door that hadn't moved. Then a voice, a voice from behind him. He couldn't make out the words, just the sound of a voice. It wasn't Mr. Stenson, he could tell that.

M immediately looked across to the table where Mrs. Cross was, but she wasn't. The footsteps to whoever the voice belonged to were walking across the tiled floor in front of the servery. As the footsteps got louder, the voice got clearer.

"We've got to clean the camel house out, then the giraffes, then it's feeding time for sea lions and otters", the voice instructed.

It was a female voice, but not an old voice.

M tucked himself right in the corner, so he was obscured by the carousel. Only his black trainers and the bottom of his navy jeans could be seen, but only if you looked closely at the base of the carousel. M was able to see through some empty wire pockets, where leaflets hadn't been refilled. He held his breath as the footsteps passed the carousel. He daren't move. As the voice passed the carousel towards the door, the footsteps stopped. M could just make out it was the lady who looked after the aviary, where all the birds were kept. She was a lot older than M, but not as old as his Mum or Mrs. Cross, he knew her name, but just couldn't think of it right now. Motionless M peered through, afraid to breath, afraid to move. M guessed she was the same age as Miss Rawson, his teacher, and in his mind had the figure of twenty five.

"Squaaaaaaaaaawwwk".

The shriek of bird made M jump slightly, not a huge jump, but just a little one that he was able to control and not touch the carousel.

"Water!" came the female voice.

The footsteps backtracked towards the servery. M breathed again, heard a door open and then pushed shut again. It closed with a low thud, which he recognised, and click, which he didn't. Then the footsteps came towards him again. He heard the twist and break of a seal of water bottle. Peeking through the carousel, he saw the young lady pass, then make for the door that had opened.

As M leaned slightly to his left and looked around the carousel, he saw the door was open, and the lady stood in the door holding it open with her right foot, as if waiting for someone to follow. His gaze lifted. She was wearing the boots all the keepers wore, green socks, bare legs, green shorts and a green long sleeved shirt. She had no hat on and her hair was in a ponytail. She look a drink of water straight from the bottle. Perched on her shoulder was a large grey parrot.

M tried to remember what it was but couldn't. He was too intent on not breathing or moving as she was only a about three maybe four metres away from him. He was sure he wouldn't have been able to remember his own name at this point, let alone the name of a species of parrot.

After what seemed like a few minutes, although it was really only seconds, the lady moved away from the door and out of the café, leaving the door to close on its own, which it did silently. As it closed it met with the other door, opened inwards slightly, closed, opened outwards a little, then the two doors came together.

M breathed again and he felt his whole body relax. He moved to his right a little, leaning rather than stepping, so he could see the windows. He saw her and the parrot walking past the Lions, Elephants, Penguins, zoo sign, Meercats, camels, and sealions windows. She was gone.

There was movement again, this time inside the café, and at floor level. Mrs. Cross crawled out from underneath a table, nudging a chair as she emerged. M decided it was safe to come out of his hiding place, got on all fours and crawled to her.

"That was close" he said, almost breathless.

He was surprised at his breathlessness, as he knew he hadn't been running. The hiding, not breathing and tension of the last five minutes or so had taken his normal breathing and left him panting. Mrs. Cross had no words, instead she just blew out puffing her cheeks, which M interpreted as a "Yes, that was very close".

M turned on his knees and scrambled quickly to the servery and looked for a door that might close with a thud.

"Where are you going? Come back!", whispered Mrs. Cross.

He crawled towards the till, turned to face Mrs. Cross and gave her a thumbs up. He ventured around the back of the servery, where he thought he'd heard the girl's footsteps going. He'd never been around this side before, but he was met with a row of stainless steel doors below the counter, with vertical handles close together.

M pulled both handles towards him, opening doors. The hinges to each door were on opposite sides. He opened them carefully so as to minimise the noise it might make. Both doors opened to opened to one fridge, and it was full of bottles of water. The fridges were still working, and they were really cold.

M took two bottles and let the fridge doors close. They both closed on their own quite quickly and shut with a low thud and a click of the handles, as he'd heard before. It was the same low thud on closing as his Mum's fridge at home. That's where he's heard it before.

It was difficult to crawl, as he found out, with two bottles of Buxton water in his hands. He found out when he couldn't put any weight on his hands because he was holding them. His left elbow buckled, and he almost fell flat on his nose.

He decided he'd do a walking run, bent at the waist to keep low, back to Mrs. Cross where he presented her with one of the bottles. They hadn't had a drink all morning, and any they had brought, including M's two cartons were still in Mrs. Cross' car. They both unscrewed the lids and drank. Mrs. Cross sipped, M glugged and almost choked. He managed to stop but a little of the water did come out of his nose, which stung a little it made him screw his face up.

"Did you see her?", M asked Mrs. Cross, who nodded between sips of water.

"More importantly, did you hear her?", retorted Mrs. Cross screwing the cap back on the water bottle.

"I heard her say water", said M, trying to think if she's said anything else. He was sure she hadn't. "I heard a squawk, which made me jump, then she said water", confirmed M.

"No, she squawked, and the parrot said water!", corrected Mrs. Cross.

"You mean like...?". M hadn't finished before Mrs. Cross interrupted.

"Exactly like Mr. Stenson and Charlie", she said.

All M could say in response to this was, "Oh boy!".

"It's no wonder the zoo is closed if all the keepers can't talk", she said, almost to herself, but loud enough for M to think she was talking to him.

"Camel house, giraffes, sea lions and otters", M blurted.

"I beg your pardon?", Mrs. Cross asked M, a little puzzled at his outburst.

"Before she got to the till, they said clean the camel house out, then the giraffes, then it's feeding time for sea lions and otters".

M took out a leaflet from his pocket that he'd taken from the carousel he was hiding behind. It was a one page printed leaflet that contained feeding times for the animals at the zoo. At these times visitors were invited to come to the enclosures and see the various animals being fed by the keepers.

"What's that?" asked Mrs. Cross

"The feeding timetable", M told her studying it.

"Brilliant!!", said an excited Mrs. Cross, "That's it!", she exclaimed further.

M had the realisation almost a second later.

"Of course!", he said, almost as excited, "If we know where the keepers are, then we can keep out of their way, or at least hide nearby".

"That's assuming they're keeping to the timetable". Mrs. Cross now sounded unsure their epiphany was a good one.

"Yes, they will", confirmed M, "I remember Mr. Stenson telling me, they always fed the animals at exactly the same time, even when the zoo was closed".

"Are you sure?"

"Yes, the animals need a routine just like a pet. That's how I remember", M exclaimed.

"It's ten fifty now, so what is due to be fed next?"

"Camels at ten forty five", M read out loud, "Giraffes at eleven fifteen, sea lions at eleven forty five".

Mrs. Cross frisked herself, checking all her pockets, both inside her jacket and out.

"All my pens are in the car", she muttered.

"There may be one over there", and with that, M made a commando style dash for the till area. Mrs. Cross didn't have time to tell M to stay close or not to go over there. M was like a whippet!

No sooner had M got to the till, he'd found not one pen, but three, and with all of them in one hand, he commando crawled back to Mrs. Cross. She turned the leaflet over and scribbled to make sure the first pen worked. It did, and with that she placed the other two in her pocket, just in case.

With the leaflet now printed side up, she crossed off what animals had been fed.

"It's giraffes next. So if we can make it to the sea lions for a quarter to twelve and hide somewhere there", Mrs Cross suggested. She drew a star next to sea lions and otters.

M looked at the list, and at the star she'd drawn.

"The otters aren't far away from the sea lions", M commented.

He was right, the otters were in the next water enclosure, and between the two was a bridge and a tunnel. If you walked over the bridge you could see the sea lions on one side and the otters on the other. If you walked under the bridge, there were very thick windows that looked into each water filled enclosure. On one side you could watch the sea lions playing underwater, through the other you could watch the otters. It was very clever, and M could remember Mr. Stenson telling him how they'd come up with the idea, and how complicated it had been to build.

"We could hide under the bridge", said M. He was mustering all he'd been told in the past by Mr. Stenson on his family trips.

"We'd be caught easily", Mrs. Cross replied.

"No", exclaimed M, "They don't use the tunnel to take the food to the sea lions or the otters. They don't even use the bridge".

"It may change when nobody is in the zoo". Mrs Cross was trying to second guess any remote possibility that things may have changed, and to ensure they weren't discovered.

With all the food now prepared for all the animals, Mr. Stenson was now in the office doing some paperwork. He was sat at his computer typing frantically. He stopped, lifted a Chalford Zoo mug, looked into it and screeched! Charlie the chimp who was sat in the chair next to him, minding his own business and self-grooming his left arm, jumped with fright at the screech.

"ooh ooh ooh ooh-hoo ooh-hoo", shouted Mr. Stenson, waving the empty mug in the air.

"I'd love another water", answered Charlie, "But please don't wave your mug in the air like that. If you let go you could do some damage to something or someone", he continued.

Mr. Stenson stopped still. He grunted at Charlie.

"Apology accepted", replied Charlie.

There was an awkward three second silence between them, only broken by another small grunt from Mr. Stenson, who then got up and made his way, mug in hand, to the small kitchen area.

Charlie remained in the office and continued grooming. He shuffled into a more crouched position on the chair to start on his right arm. As he shuffled a remote control device that was on the chair fell to the floor, button side down. Charlie looked at the floor, looked at the remote, then instead of picking it up he did what any other chimp would do. Simply ignored the device, remote or not, on the floor and went back to the all-important grooming of his right arm. He looked closely at his arm as he groomed but was distracted by a flickering on the computer screen, which he hadn't noticed earlier, when Mr. Stenson had been sat there. He looked at the screen.

The work Mr. Stenson had been doing was now gone, and had been replaced by CCTV screens, six of them, but all changing to a different view every five seconds. It was this changing of camera views that were the cause of the flickering. He was mesmerised by this and stared, completely forgetting about the whole grooming of his arm.

There were cameras all over the zoo. Those in the animal's enclosures to keep a watch on their behaviour and welfare. Those in and around the zoos pathways and roads to keep an eye on visitors for their safety and security. There were also cameras around the entrances and perimeter, mainly for security, but also for queue control and staff security.

There had never been an instance at the zoo where the keepers had to act on anything untoward at the main entrance. Mr. Stenson's staff kept the queues, even on busy days, well managed, in good humour and well controlled. From the screens it was difficult to say how many cameras there actually were dotted around the zoo.

As the screens flickered while Mr. Stenson was in the kitchen Charlie could see in the elephant house, the giraffe house, the large reptile house. These cameras were infrared, and at night the view in the dark was as good as it was in the day.

Charlie watched the flickering as the views changed. From in the enclosures to the deserted main entrance, from inside the animals sleeping quarters to the empty pathways and roads. Back to the enclosures they changed to the outside of the café and then to the delivery entrance.

Charlie could see the meercats standing to attention on the lookout for predators, even though there weren't any. Or were they looking up at their perimeter wall wondering why there were no visitors looking that them, looking at them, watching them standing to attention. Wondering why there were no children standing to attention in a similar fashion mimicking them standing to attention, just moving just their heads quickly from side to side.

Charlie then realised he'd seen something that shouldn't have been there on the previous screen. Now he had to wait until it was that cameras turn to show up on screen again. As a chimp, he had no idea that he could use the remote device to control what views he saw, or that he could make one camera full screen, rather than the six small flickering screens he was now staring at.

Mr. Stenson came back into the room with his mug and a red plastic cup. He placed his mug, now refilled with hot coffee onto a Chalford Zoo coaster on the desk to the right of the keyboard. He turned and offered Charlie the other cup and made a low grunt. Charlie smelled the water and took a sip.

"Much obliged", Charlie responded politely.

Again, Mr. Stenson made the low grunt and sat on his chair, swivelled around to face his computer screen. On seeing the CCTV images he swiftly turned again to Charlie, who just shrugged. Mr. Stenson then looked down at the floor and the device that had fallen below Charlie's chair. Bending from his own chair he went to retrieve the device and snorted down his nose in disapproval. He was just about to press one button or another.

"Wait", instructed Charlie, "I'm sure I saw something".

Mr. Stenson cocked his head to one side as if he hadn't understood what Charlie had said, then dismissed picking up the device and sat up to look again at the screens. They continued to flick from one view to the next. Charlie was sure he'd seen the delivery entrance camera shown in the bottom left hand screen, however as much as he stared that image didn't reappear immediately. The problem was that the screens changed randomly, so any camera view that was shown in say the top middle screen, would then appear in the bottom right. There was a pattern to the constant flicking, but it seemed to be random to Charlie. That and he wasn't that clever to be able to work it out, so he had to wait.

Mr. Stenson became impatient. He put both hands on each arm of the swivel chair, lifted his bottom off and brought his feet onto the chair. He then bared his teeth and screeched, shaking his head violently from side to side.

"Well if you'll be patient, I'll show you. It was at the back entrance", said Charlie trying to calm his keeper.

Mr. Stenson settled himself back to a normal seated position in the chair. As he shifted his weight back to the arms to reposition his legs, the chair almost toppled and he let out another high pitched shriek. He balanced again, bent down from the chair to pick up the remote device. With a couple of presses of this button and that, the screen had changed from six cameras to one in full screen format that was changed manually. Pressing again on the buttons, the camera shot changed one by one until it was showing the view from the top of the animal feed building to the inside of the big green gates, with the small gate inset into the left hand one and the gate control to the left of that.

Mr. Stenson and Charlie studied it, but nothing looked out of the ordinary. All three gates were closed. There had been no intruder alarm that would have alerted them to any unwanted visitors, and all seemed normal. Mr. Stenson pressed again, and the full screen changed back to the six flickering ones and reached out to lift his mug to his lips. Charlies gaze was fixed on the bottom left hand box.

"There!", he said pointing frantically.

By the time Mr. Stenson had sipped, hurriedly put his drink back on the coaster, the image had changed. With the remote control still in his left hand, Mr. Stenson made the images full screen again, and flicked through the cameras one by one. It took a while, but eventually they were looking at the green gates again. The next shot was from a tree situated about 12 metres outside the zoo perimeter wall. This looked directly at the first intercom. This would show the face of any driver that pulled up to gain authorised access by a member of staff.

At the next screen, the camera was pointing at and showed the outside of the green gates where the other intercom, without a camera was. This was the intercom where M and Mrs. Cross heard the cackle laughter come from.

"There!" shouted Charlie pointing again, which made Mr. Stenson jump again.

And there is was, Mrs. Cross' car still there, almost looking abandoned at the roadside. Mr. Stenson pressed another button on the control that paused the image. They both stared at the screen, Mr. Stenson in his chair, Charlie a little further back on his chair. Both bared their teeth, but only Mr. Stenson left his chair and proceeded to jump up and down on the spot, screeching and chattering, and pointing at the screen.

"I don't know whose car it is", replied Charlie, obviously understanding the ranting chimp-like noises being made by the zoo owner, who continued to chatter and screech.

"Oh yes!", exclaimed Charlie, "The woman and boy that were with the delivery man this morning. Of course. But why would they leave their car there?"

More jumping, more screeching, more chattering from the man in the green shirt, who promptly stopped, got back on his chair and took a sip of his coffee. It was almost like he'd forgotten he was acting like a chimp. Instead he just stared at the screen over his cup as he drank.

In the café, Mrs. Cross and M were carefully planning their next move, still studying the sheet with the feeding times printed on.

"If we have our cakes now, in here, then we can make our way to the tunnel. If we go over the bridge, we're more likely to be spotted", Mrs. Cross told M.

Even though M knew the layout of the zoo like the back of his hand, he needed to make sure he knew exactly where he was going. He was loving this adventure. When he got into Mrs. Cross' car this morning he had no idea his day was going to turn out like it was doing. Although he was still worried about Mr. Stenson and the animals, this day was turning out to be one of the best days of his life. He never knew Mrs. Cross was such an adventurer too. After all he only ever saw her when he was either crossing the road to and from school, or when she called at his house to see his Mum.

He did his commando crawl back to the leaflet carousel and selected one of the maps of the zoo. Normally he's have been given one at the entrance as his Mum or Dad paid to get in. As they'd not come into the zoo by the usual entrance, no map had been presented to them by Mr. Stenson or Charlie. In actual fact nobody knew he and Mrs. Cross were in the zoo at all, although they had spotted her car outside the gates.

M crawled back to Mrs. Cross and opened the map on the floor so they could both see it clearly. With the wrong end of the pen, Mrs. Cross drew an imaginary line from the café to the sea lions water enclosure.

"That's not a good way to go", M said with some knowledge. "We'd have to go over the bridge that way".

With his index finger he drew another imaginary line from the café to the sea lions, avoiding the bridge".

"Good thinking", Mrs. Cross said agreeing with M. "It's a longer way around, but no bridge".

"We have to go out of this back door", said M pointing to the door where earlier the parrot lady had exited, "Then all around, past the kangaroos and wallabies, the meercats and tapirs".

Mrs. Cross followed M's finger on the map.

"Then cut through the birds of prey straight to the tunnel", she added.

"Exactly", confirmed M.

With that Mrs. Cross drew on the map with the correct end of the pen the route that they had both agreed.

He folded the map back up, but then had to unfold it again to be able to fold it properly. No matter how many maps of the zoo M had handled, he could never fold it back the way it should have been folded first time. He handed it to Mrs. Cross who popped it into the pocket with the pens in. She handed the pen to M who struggled to find a pocket that he was comfortable it being in. Eventually he handed it to Mrs. Cross to put in her pocket to keep the other pens and map company.

They both tucked into cake and bottled water before venturing out from the relative safety of the café.

In the office Mr. Stenson and Charlie had resigned themselves to the fact that an abandoned car was sat outside the zoo. Neither of them thought the occupants would be sneaking around the zoo unaccompanied and they hadn't paid to get in! Mr. Stenson had returned to his frantic typing, while Charlie had resumed the all-important grooming of his arms.

As M and Mrs. Cross made their way to the back door, cake wrappers binned so as not to leave any evidence they'd been in the café, Mrs. Cross stopped M in his tracks to signify she was to open the door first. M complied with the silent request and watched as his accomplice carefully opened the door.

She did her usual right, left, right looking again. She may have been illicitly sneaking around a zoo like an undercover cop with her young sidekick, but the right, left, right look before crossing a road never left her.

After ensuring the coast was clear she motioned for M to follow her over the wide walkway that ran across the back of the zoo. To the left would take them towards the main entrance, to the right towards the kangaroos and wallabies. As they exited right, just ahead a narrower path crossed. To the left would take them the shorter way, to the right would take them along the length of the café from where they'd come originally. Straight on it was, and after another right, left, right, they made their way. They weren't running fast, but they weren't walking slowly, it was somewhere in-between, a comfortable pace for both.

It wasn't long before they had left the open space of the café and picnic area and on a narrower path between two fenced enclosures. On the left were the wallabies on the right the kangaroos. The kangaroo area was open and largely treeless, whereas the wallaby pen was full of small bushes because of what each of the animals eat.

There were information signs on each of the enclosures explaining all this and other facts about the animals living and eating patterns and diets. M had read these many times before and knew some of them off by heart. He liked the way they explained things simply, specifically for children. He didn't have time to read them now, there were much more important things to concentrate on, like not being caught.

Another cross path appeared, where they had to go right. This time M did the right, left, right looking thing, and when he was sure it was safe, he that motioned to Mrs. Cross, and on they went, to the right between the wallabies and the meercats. The wallaby fence was quite high to their right, but the meercat wall on their left was relatively low, so they had to do the running walk, or the walking run slightly stooped to minimise their visibility.

Although the wall was low it was long. What they couldn't see, partly because they were keeping close to the wallaby fence was the dividing wall separating the meercats from the tapirs. As they came to the end of the fence the path went right to follow the wallaby enclosure or straight on to the end of the meercat and tapir pens, and then went either straight on or left between the tapirs on the left and flamingos on the right. Left it was and this would lead them to the tunnel where they agreed they were heading.

CHAPTER SIX: SEALS & OTTERS

Just before the tunnel stood a wooden shed-like building that was actually an ice cream kiosk. The front shutter with hinges along the top was closed, but the side door for 'staff only' was open. They both noticed this together and stopped dead in their tracks. Both put a finger to their lips each telling the other not to make a sound.

They tip-toed past, just in case any staff were in there. With no visitors in the zoo it didn't matter it was open, M thought to himself, there was nobody, except him and Mrs. Cross, that could take anything. They wouldn't steal, although M quickly reminded himself that they needed to pay for the cakes they'd had in the café, so technically it wasn't stealing.

Ten metres or so further on and they were in the tunnel. Hidden for the time being from anyone or anything that walked or drove a zoo buggy around. The bridge above was wide, which made the tunnel wide. Although, at feeding time, if you were caught in the middle when all the crowds were here, all you could see was the backs of people's heads. Or in M's case the backs of people's backs.

The mini tractors and trailers would travel over the bridge. They were used to carry the heavy feeds to the larger animals like the elephants or rhinos. M had also seen an older couple once being ferried around on a little buggy. One or both couldn't walk so well, so they were being driven around the zoo by a keeper. M thought that was a great idea. Mrs. Cross and M couldn't have used one today as it would have made too much noise and alerted suspicions straight away.

In the tunnel they both gave a huge sigh of relief as for now they were safe. They both knew they couldn't stay here for long, but long enough to come up with the next part of their plan and to consult the map again. The tunnel was about twenty feet long. They knew they hadn't been followed in, but M wanted to make sure there was no-one at the other end.

"Wait here", he told Mrs. Cross.

"Where are... ", Mrs, Cross started.

"Back in a minute", reassured M, and he set off to the far end.

From the other end, you could look out, along the path where it crossed a road. There was a zebra crossing, so that visitors could cross safely to the other side. The buggies and tractors always stopped here as the visitors were the important people and were always allowed to cross. As soon as M saw the crossing a short distance ahead, he smiled, because if you crossed there, on the other side was the zebra enclosure. A perfectly placed zebra crossing.

His smile was interrupted by the sound of an engine. It was in the distance but gradually getting louder and louder. He ducked back into the safety of the tunnel, keeping his eyes on the crossing. The engine was either on that road or on the road that went over the tunnel. It was possibly bringing the fish for the sea lions and otters feeding time.

As M could clearly hear the vehicle now, it wasn't going to come over the bridge, and he was aware that it would be passing his line of vision any moment. He cowered against the left wall of the tunnel. The driver probably wouldn't notice him where he was, but he would see them. He held his breath. His eyes firmly fixed on the crossroads ahead, his back almost fused to the wall, the motor was as loud as it was going to get before passing him and then would get quieter as it put more distance between him and it.

Here is comes, here it comes. There it is, there it is. There it goes, there it went across the roads that formed part of the network of paths and roads around the zoo. That wasn't what he was expecting at all. Not a buggy, not a mini tractor, although thinking about it, and now that he'd seen it, it didn't sound like a buggy or a tractor. It was a white van with black patches on it. It seemed familiar to M, and he couldn't help thinking he'd seen it before.

It was one of those things, like when you see someone you think you know and you have to try to put their face into a scenario where it face fits so you can put a name to that person and know where you know them from. It was the same with the van, he just had to put the van somewhere in his mind so that he could know where he knew it from. That was frustrating. His heart was racing from hiding, and all he could think about was how hard and fast his blood was being pumped around his small body.

"Pssssst", he hissed to Mrs. Cross walking quickly back to her.

"Psssst yourself", she hissed back.

"Just saw a van", he said almost panting, even though he hadn't been running.

"What kind of van?"

"Black and white. I'm sure I know it from somewhere"

"Probably here", said Mrs. Cross trying to state the obvious.

M put the van at the zoo in his mind, but it didn't fit the mental jigsaw he had created. Almost immediately he dismissed the notion that he'd seen the van at the zoo before and shook his head at Mrs. Cross to dignify it. That didn't appease his frustration, but there were more important things to think about now. The feeding of the sea lions and otters was imminent.

"What's the time?", M asked.

"Twenty five to twelve"

"Ten minutes to feeding", M stated, remembering the times from the feeding sheet.

"We need to be very quiet in here, there's a bit of an echo and I don't know how it travels out of here", Mrs. Cross instructed.

While they'd been hiding, whispering and car spotting, well M had, they had failed to notice the goings on in the water enclosures on either side. To Mrs. Cross' right and M's left the sea lions were playing gleefully to their two man audience. Although Mrs. Cross was not a man, the sea lions were probably ignorant of this. Nevertheless they swam back and forth behind the thick glass.

Every time they passed the window of their world the sea lions seemed to look and smile. M smiled back. The sea lions were one of his favourite animals to watch at the zoo. Feeding time was always fun as on special occasions someone from the crowd was invited in to help feed them. If a kid had a birthday party at the zoo, that kid was invited as a treat.

It had happened to M once on his eighth birthday, and even though he didn't have a party there, his Mum had told Mr. Stenson that they were planning a birthday trip to the zoo. Mr. Stenson had agreed that M could feed the sea lions on their visit. It was a complete surprise, but he felt very special that day as the whole crowd that had gathered to watch were looking at him throwing fish to the sea lions. The keepers name was Jane, and she, together with Mr. Stenson, had called M's name over the microphone she was wearing, telling everyone it was his birthday, he was eight and he wanted to be a zookeeper.

M liked Jane and from that day on she always smiled whenever she saw him. M always noticed that whenever he saw her, she was always wearing her microphone. He always thought she looked like a pop star about to perform a concert.

He got a huge clap from the crowd that day. His Mum and Dad knew about the treat and stood near to the gate which Mr. Stenson had opened to let him in. He could still remember how special he felt, and he could still remember how his hands stank of fish afterwards. Even though he washed them, rinsed them, dried them and washed, rinsed and dried them about five times that day, he could still smell fish for ages after.

It was sort of his own fault, Jane had given him some gloves to wear, but they were so big, after he had thrown the first fish, he put his hand so deep into the bucket, bits of fish and fish juice had leaked over the top of the gloves and made his hands smell.! Yuck!!

In the opposite windows, made of the same think glass on M's right and Mrs. Cross' left were the otters. They were also swimming to and fro past the glass. Summersaulting, diving and generally playing, paying no attention to either of their two spectators. M smiled and returned his attention to the sea lions.

"They know it's almost feeding time", M told Mrs. Cross.

As they watched the playful marine animals swimming, smiling, they were getting faster and faster past the glass windows. Under any other circumstances, M would be running from one window to the next and back again, following the sea lions and almost playing with them.

He envied how well they swam, and how slick they were. He wished he could swim as well as that, but he was only in group six of his swimming classes at Chalford swimming pool. Even if he was a better swimmer, he would be no match for the sea lions either in this zoo or in the wild. As they both watched and M envied, they both became almost tranced by the black sleek creatures darting through the water, holding their breath with relative ease.

Their trance was broken by the sound of a sharp high pitched whistle. As if by magic the sea lions disappeared. It was as if the shutters had gone down and they were obscured from public view. Mrs. Cross jumped at the whistle and looked at M with a very worried look on her face.

M laughed a little, although it was more a nervous laugh than one where he found something funny.

"Feeding time whistle", M announced.

Within seconds of the whistle blowing, a dead herring had entered the water from above, it appeared on the other side of the glass, and sank slowly towards the bottom of the huge tank. The dead fish got about halfway down the glass when from out of what seemed like nowhere a black creature appeared and 'gulp', the fish was gone, as was the creature. One of the sea lions had followed the fish through the air above the water, watched where it had entered and snapped it up. No sooner had that seal disappeared another appeared, just seconds too late.

Another whistle, another fish and another seal, just as quick appeared, disappeared. Their gaze was firmly fixed at the middle window, where it seemed all the action was happening. What M and Mrs. Cross couldn't see was all the other fish being thrown into the pool from above. They were entering the water in other parts of the pool not visible from where they were. Had they been on the bridge they would have seen the sea lions jumping out of the water catching fish even before they'd hit the water. They were very quick.

What they hadn't noticed was the one seal in the left hand window. It didn't seem bothered with any fish. Instead it was swimming up and down in that window, catching breath as it surfaced to be able to duck down again. Maybe it was catching fish above the surface, or getting them after they'd hit the water, before they came into view of their underwater spectators. Up it ascended, and came down for a fourth or fifth time, glanced at the two humans in the tunnel, then it was gone, like a magic trick, just gone.

There was then one heck of a hullabaloo above the surface.

Jane knew their names. To M, they all looked the same, a sea lion was a sea lion, was a sea lion. He remembered Jane telling him to throw a fish to Angie, then to Walter. It's a good job she pointed, and even then, he just threw the fish on his eighth birthday in the general direction of where she was pointing. He'd gone home that day hugely elated that he'd helped feed the sea lions. He'd also gone home wondering why on days like that they didn't put name tags on the sea lions, so birthday boys and girls knew which was which. Even when one seal came up on the sloping entrance to the water, and Jane had said, "Give Martha a fish", if he saw Martha again, he wouldn't have known it was her.

As well as wondering why they didn't give name tags to them, there was the two day exercise M had given himself. He had tasked himself whilst in the bath, at the age of eight and one day to come up with a way of making name tags or labels for sea lions. He'd used paper and garden twine to go around their necks. The paper got soggy in the water and all the ink smudged and ran, so you couldn't read them.

The next night (aged eight and two days) he'd used sticky labels with indelible ink. He'd stuck these to himself, but they got soggy, and he'd lost some leg hairs when he'd tried to get them off. That really hurt, but the ink hadn't run. He tried the same on one of Chloe's teddies. Once again, the ink hadn't run, but he had completely ruined the teddy. It had got waterlogged.

For about an hour afterwards, when you pressed its foot to make it say, "I love you", it sounded like it was talking under water. Then it stopped working altogether, and it took a whole two weeks to dry out. Mum had even had to take the teddy, with Chloe, to the consultation room at the local chemist, only to be told it had a bad case of laryngitis. So he dismissed the idea of labels for sea lions.

M heard Jane's voice, then it stopped, then came the frantic barking of a sea lion, quickly followed by the hullabaloo of all the other sea lions joining in. Whatever was going on up there had obviously got the animals all excited or all scared. As well as M not knowing their names, he also didn't know the difference between excited sea lions and scared sea lions. Something he needed to know if he wanted to be a zookeeper. Now wasn't the time to learn that difference.

It was one seal in particular that caught the attention of both M and Mrs. Cross. It sounded louder than the other sea lions, almost electronic, no that wasn't the word. Amplified was the word! That was it, it sounded amplified. At that exact moment, M and Mrs. Cross looked at each other. Together they both said at exactly the same time, "It's on the loudspeaker!!".

Neither of them had remembered they were in hiding, and neither of them had whispered. Fortunately the noise from above drowned their shouting out, even though they were in a tunnel and it echoed a little. As both of them realised they had shouted louder than either of them had meant to, there was silence in the tunnel, not from above though, it was all still going on up there. The barking of all the sleek black marine mammals was enough to drown a football crowd shouting and celebrating after their team had scored.

The barking of the sea lions was almost deafening, and both the intrepid adventurers were more than curious as to what had started it. They had two choices. They could either stay where they were, or they could make a run for it, try to see what the commotion was about, then make for another safe place. Mrs. Cross took the map from her pocket, unfolded and laid it on the ground.

"If we go out of here the way we came in, left then right past the bat house and into the nature reserve. We could hide there".

"Hide!", exclaimed M

"Yes, hide"

"No, there is a hide in the nature bit, where you can watch the birds".

"Brilliant", added Mrs. Cross, "All we have to do is get out of here without being seen"

"If Jane is feeding the sea lions, and they're making a noise, maybe she won't see us"

"Possibly"

While studying the map, they were unaware of the eyes that were studying them. Behind the glass, that one sea lion was as still interested in the hiding twosome as it had been from their arrival.

"We need to move now. When we get to the reserve, we can decide what to do next and how to help".

"That's what we came for in the first place", M reminded her.

"Out, left, right, bat house, nature reserve", Mrs. Cross recited, folding the map up. She did it first time, which impressed M.

"Follow me, keep close".

They nodded at each other that they were both ready, and with that nod, they made a run for it. Out of the tunnel they way they'd come in. Suddenly they were in full view of all the sea lions, and Jane. Luckily, Jane had her back to them, but not for long. The beady eyed sea lion that had taken an unhealthy interest in them down below made a dart for the surface as soon as they had started running.

As the sea lion surfaced, it exhaled, then inhaled, caught its breath.

"There they are!", it shouted.

M and Mrs. Cross ran along the wall that held the dark murky water from spilling out. The right hand turn before the bat house seemed to get further away the more they ran towards it, like one of those weird optical illusions.

Jane turned to face them, as always, microphone clipped over one ear with the mouthpiece attached, which just covered the right hand side of her mouth. She pointed at the two intruders. As she pointed, her hand following their path, that same sea lion swam almost at the speed of sound towards Jane.

"We've been well and truly spotted", Mrs. Cross tried to shout behind her. There was no point in whispering now.

M was about to answer but was cut short by Jane... Barking like a sea lion, which was immediately amplified by the microphone and the four of five speakers that were dotted about the area. She also clapped her hands in front of her. Normally Jane would have been telling visitors all about the animals she looked after and fed, their natural habitat, hunting and eating habits, all that stuff. Today, she was barking! Of course when she barked, all the other sea lions barked resulting in yet another commotion and almost deafening noise.

Within seconds, and moments before they'd reached the right hander at the bat house, that sea lion had left the water and had sidled up to Jane with almost Olympic gymnast precision. Jane took the walkie-talkie from a holster in her belt and held it to the sea lions' mouth.

"We've spotted intruders at Sea Lion Sanctuary, currently heading for Bat Colony Canyon".

CHAPTER SEVEN: THE RESERVE & CAFÉ

Back in the office, Mr. Stenson and Charlie heard the call and scrambled into action, both leaving their respective chairs spinning. Out of the office and into a waiting buggy they both ran.

In the parrot house Josie, the keeper M had seen in the café heard the same call. She dropped the apple she was preparing and ran to the door. Behind her the grey parrot left its perch and landed itself expertly on the running keeper's shoulder, gripping the epaulette of her shirt so as not to fall off mid-run.

With the bat house behind them the human intruders, which is what the sea lion had called them, were a mere five steps away from the nature reserve. It wasn't a huge reserve, but a small cleverly designed area with windy paths through high bushes, trees and shrubs. There was a small clearing at the far end where the hide was. This allowed people to watch as the wild birds came to feed from the various bird feeders that were scattered about the clearing. The windy paths made it seem bigger than it was.

Mr. Stenson and Charlie had reached the sanctuary where Jane and the sea lion where waiting. Jane was just outside of the small gate; the sea lion was inside.

Mr. Stenson screeched and jumped with hands flailing.

Jane barked and clapped her hands.

Mr. Stenson stopped and looked at Jane, she looked at Mr. Stenson and Charlie, then they all turned to look at the sea lion.

Moments later, Josie and the African Grey arrived. She jumped off the small tractor she'd ridden on.

Mr. Stenson screeched, jumped and waved arms about.

Jane barked and clapped hands.

Josie squawked and sort of bobbed up and down. Then she too turned to the sea lion.

"This is getting us nowhere" it said, "We have two intruders, a boy and a woman".

Mr. Stenson chattered a little and ended with a screech and then blew a raspberry.

"It must be the same two we saw earlier", announced Charlie, "Their car is parked outside the back gates".

Josie squawked, chirruped and squawked, then did a delightful wolf-whistle.

"We've been riding around all morning and haven't seen anyone", said the parrot to everyone.

"They were heading towards the bats", the sea lion told them. "I can't come, but you're better splitting up. You'll have a better chance of catching them". The sea lion told the other five.

Josie immediately chirruped again, with the customary sort of bobbing.

"Point of order", it said, "Would I be best circling from above and reporting back?"

Charlie ooh'd and aah'd and jumped, then bared as many teeth as he could at Mr. Stenson, who replied in a similar way.

"Splendid idea", exclaimed Charlie.

With that the man and chimp ran off towards the bats, the girl and parrot ran off past the flamingos towards the café. The parrot then leapt off her shoulder and soared over head seeing what it could see.

Huddled in the hide, M and Mrs. Cross were out of breath and slightly sweating. The hide was made from wood, like a big garden shed but with only a front, two sides and half a roof. The two shorter sides were solid, and the front had small horizontal slits to look through. Some were high for tall visitors, and some were lower for short visitors, and there were platforms for those even shorter to stand on. That was in case they couldn't see through the lower slits. The half a roof was from the front to halfway across the shorter sides. It was decorated with pictures of some common and some not so common birds that visited.

"I haven't run that fast in years", panted Mrs. Cross

M smiled, he had run that fast only recently on school sports day, but that was in a straight line across a sports field, not a windy nature reserve.

Mrs. Cross passed the bottle of water to M. It wasn't as cold and refreshing as it had been straight from the fridge, even so, it did stop the back of his throat stinging from being so dry from running and panting.

"We can't spend the rest of the day running around the zoo. We came here to find out why it was closed".

"I think we know that", said M, catching his breath, "How can he run a zoo if he can't talk normally?"

Mrs. Cross looked deep in thought.

"He talked like a chimp, she talked like a parrot and Jane talked like a sea lion", said M, attempting to make some sense of it all.

"And all the animals they look after talk like their keepers used to do", stated Mrs. Cross attempting to join the puzzle together.

"Of course you can't open a zoo with all that going on", she added.

"It's like", started M.

He was cut short by the sound of flapping above, which then stopped, but was quickly followed by a hopping sound on the roof. They both looked up to where the half roof met the canopy of leaves above.

"Ah-ha", said M.

"Ah-ha?"

"The talking sea lion must have seen us in the tunnel", muttered M.

"And now the parrot had found us", said Mrs. Cross looking up. It flew off immediately.

Mrs. Cross checked her phone.

"No signal here, we need to get back to the café, it has signal and wi-fi", she told M.

"If the parrot thinks we're here, we can be in the café by the time they get here if we leave now".

No other words were necessary, they were off, following the trails of the reserve back, out and back towards the café. M lead them the long way to avoid bat houses and sea lions.

In the café Mrs. Cross made straight for the fridge for water, one for her and one for M, and more wrapped cakes. They sat on the floor near to the table where the bottles were. There were even more now, and some other wrappers.

"I have no idea what's going on here", said Mrs. Cross between sips of water.

"I think I do. Got a pen?".

M wrote on the back of a new feeding leaflet he'd snatched on the way in.

"Mr. Stenson and Charlie, Jane and the sea lion and Jodie and the parrot", he spoke as he wrote, "They've all been swapped with the most intelligent and vocal animals that they look after".

"I get that M, but why?"

"That I don't know"

"I had a friend once that was made to think they were a chicken, but never anything like this"

"How", questioned M inquisitively.

"Hypnosis. He was put…", Mrs. Cross couldn't finish.

"In a trance?", because M finished her sentence for her.

"Of course", continued M, "They've all been hypnotised!!" He sounded euphoric.

"Can you hypnotise animals?"

"That van! I know where I've seen that van before"

"What van?"

"The white van I saw from the far end of the tunnel. It's the same van that comes to train Mrs. Spooner's dog".

"Training a dog it one thing. This is something else altogether".

"But it isn't, she's training her dog not to bark, so if she can train dogs not to bark, can she train other animals not to make their noises?"

"hmmmm", pondered Mrs. Cross.

"So why else would she be here?". M was quite engrossed in his findings and found them all perfectly plausible.

"I don't…" Again Mrs. Cross was prevented from continuing.

It wasn't M who interrupted this time, but doors, two to be exact, at either end of the café.

Mr. Stenson ran one door in jumping and ooh-ooh-ing, Jane came in the other barking and clapping, and Josie squawked, wolf-whistled and did that sort of bobbing up and down thing.

M and Mrs. Cross were stunned with startlement (if that's a word), and then scared. Not for their lives but scared all the same.

"W..W.. We're not here to hurt you", stuttered M bravely.

Charlie looked at Sea Lion Girl who looked at Parrot Girl who looked at Charlie.

Mr. Stenson ooh'd bared his teeth and raised one hand in the air and shook a limp wristed hand.

"And we're not here to hurt you", said Charlie, getting to his feet. Mr. Stenson continued his ooh-ooh-ing and stuff. Charlie translated, as he'd done earlier over the gate.

"You're trespassing and you've stolen", he pointed to the water and cakes.

"We are going to pay for these", Mrs. Cross added nervously, looking at the water and the cakes thinking there was no point trying to hide them now.

"Never-the-less, trespassing is trespassing, and stealing is stealing".

"Don't you miss all the visitors?", it was M who interjected, addressing Charlie, but the question was open to all three.

There was a moments silence, broken only by Josie with a very loud and inappropriate wolf-whistle. Everyone, including Charlie looked at her but said nothing. She blushed.

M's tummy rumbled, which in the silence of the room sounded like a distant earthquake. Mrs. Cross looked at her watch. It was twelve twenty five.

Mr. Stenson smiled at the rumbling noise. M just smiled back, unaware of what was happening right before his eyes. It was Mrs. Cross that noticed Josie's blush and Mr. Stenson's smile.

"M's right Rob", she said directly to Mr. Stenson, "Don't you miss the visitors?"

She took M's hand and gently pulled him towards her and whispered through the corner of her mouth.

"Whatever's wrong with them is wearing off. Keep talking to them"

M sipped water from the bottle, feeling guilty after being accused of stealing it, and choked as the clear liquid caught the back of his throat. He'd tried to speak whilst drinking, and that was never a good idea. Without warning there was a burst of music and Taylor Swift's voice emerged from Mrs. Cross' pocket.

"Shake it off, Shake it off".

Mrs. Cross cautiously took her phone from her pocket. It was a message from M's Mum making sure they were enjoying their day, and if they'd had lunch. Mrs. Cross didn't reply.

It was Josie that hummed the tune back to them.

M was standing on Mrs. Cross. Left, and as he looked at her, he thought he saw a figure pass the lion window of the café. He was about to dismiss the vision, when the door was flung open. In walked a very tall lady, older than Mrs. Cross, dressed in all dark green, except for an orange scarf tied around her forehead, knotted at the back to keep her longish jet black hair off her face, and a green camouflage backpack on her left shoulder. M thought she looked like a teenage ninja turtle.

"We're late for our appointment!", the woman announced, walking towards the group of keepers.

"Appointment?", questioned Mrs. Cross.

The woman looked towards her, quite startled, as she hadn't noticed them.

The woman looked at her watch, looked at the keepers, then back at the extra two, M and Mrs. Cross.

"I've been helping the zoo", the woman explained nervously, "w..w..with some animal behaviour issues".

At that moment M heard a loud 'click' in his head, about the same volume as his earlier tummy rumble. No-one else heard the click though. This was the woman who drove the van, who came to Mrs. Spooner's house, who was training her dog to stop barking.

"It's you!", exclaimed M, once again mouth working before brain was in gear. He had no idea what he was going to say next, so brain braked, and mouth stopped.

Mr. Stenson screeched and jumped, which prompted Charlie to do the same, and Josie and the parrot to squawk and do that sort of bobbing up and down thing. Jane barked but didn't clap. There was an awful commotion going on in the café.

"Please", shouted the woman, attempting to silence the menagerie.

M thought it sounded like the first day back at school after a half term or the summer holidays. Everyone talking over everyone telling everyone about their out of school adventures.

M clapped twice, "One, two, three, look at me". M had no idea why he'd done this. He just remembered his teacher, Miss Rawson doing it!

The keepers and animals fell silent at M's interjection, and all eyes were trained on him and him alone.

"Thank you", uttered the woman in black, but nobody paid any attention to her, which only served to irritate her.

Mr. Stenson bared his teeth but didn't screech. Josie sort of bobbed but didn't squawk. Jane clapped twice. Then all three looked at each other totally wondering what they were doing in the café.

The woman in black looked on in horror as Mr. Stenson, Josie and Jane seemed no longer to act like the animals they cared for, but as people. With M and Mrs. Cross in the same room she was unable to do her 'training'.

Mr. Stenson looked across, "Hello M, nice to see you again. Jo, how are you?"

M gave a huge smile as he was once again recognised, and Jo ran to Mr. Stenson and gave him a huge hug.

"Good to have you back Rob", she told him.

"Back?" asked Mr. Stenson, puzzled.

The woman in black turned and made a bee line for the door.

"Not so fast", shouted Mr. Stenson, "Charlie, the door".

Charlie screeched and ran to the door before the woman could reach it and blocked her way.

"Josie, call the police, we have a trespasser".

Later that day, the three keepers, M and Mrs. Cross were sat in the zoo office with tea, cakes and squash for M.

"This last week has been a complete blur to us", announced Mr. Stenson.

"If it wasn't for you two, who knows where we'd be", added Jane.

"Squawwwwwk", said Josie, "Only joking", she laughed.

They all laughed!

"I don't know how to thank you both", Mr. Stenson said emotionally to M and Mrs. Cross.

"If it wasn't for you two intervening, we'd be out of business and the zoo would have closed permanently", he told them.

"The animals would have suffered and have had to be rehomed. Goodness knows where they would have ended up", Josie added, just as emotionally

Mr. Stenson stood up and gave Mrs. Cross another huge hug. "Thank you, Jo." Then he turned to M and held out his hand. M accepted and they shook hands. Mr. Stenson pulled M towards him and hugged him very tightly.

"You're always welcome to the zoo M, and to say thank you for all your help, I'd like to give you this". He produced an envelope for M and handed it to him.

"This is a free pass for life. You and your family are never to pay to get in the zoo ever again".

It was M's turn to get emotional, a free pass forever to his all-time favourite place of all time was the most amazing gift ever.

Mrs Cross had dropped M off at home and taken herself back to her own house after a brief chat with M's Mum.

M's Mum was emptying his bag.

"You didn't eat your lunch M!"

"No", he replied, "It was a pretty busy day"

"Are you going to tell me about it then? Jo said you had a bit of an adventure".

"I'll wait until Dad gets home".

M left the kitchen, with his envelope and made his way upstairs to his room. He felt tired, looked at the photos on his wall and sat on his bed.

M was woken by Chloe, who thought it would be a good idea to bound into the room pretending to be a chimp. M woke up with a start, and immediately clapped.

"One, two, three, all eyes on me"

Chloe just laughed, "You're not a teacher".

Mum and Dad came in and saw a bleary eyed M looking a little embarrassed at his outburst to Chloe.

"Mum, Dad, you'll never guess what happened" he blurted, "Mr. Stenson was a chimp and Charlie talked, and we had to hide in the tunnel and a sea lion saw us and Mrs. Cross stole cakes and water, and...", he started to trip over his words.

Chloe burst out laughing, "You've been dreaming", she giggled and ran out.

M looked at Mum and Dad, who shook their heads.

"It wasn't a dream was it?" he asked them both.

"Mrs. Cross has told us all about it", said Dad, "How you had to sneak into the zoo, with the help of a driver called Stu".

"And how you helped save the zoo from closing for good", added Mum.

"It seems young man, you've had a pretty adventurous day. No wonder you're so tired", said Dad.

"Mr. Stenson has been on the phone telling us all about it too", Mum told him, "It seems the owner of Camblington zoo was jealous of Mr. Stenson's success, and wanted to put him out of business"

"He got Wendy Watson, the animal behaviour person to go to Chalford Zoo, change the behaviour of the keepers and the animals, so they couldn't open. He planned to slowly take the other animals to his zoo", Dad explained.

"If it wasn't for you and Mrs. Cross getting involved, he'd have got away with it. The Watson woman's behaviour hypnosis only lasted a day, so she visited at the same time every day for her sessions to keep them hypnotised", Mum explained further.

"But after ten days it would have been weekly, and after a month all Mr. Stenson's animals would have been taken to Camblington zoo", stated Dad.

"We're so proud of you M"

M felt proud too, knowing that he hadn't just woken from a dream adventure.

There was a cry from outside M's bedroom window.

"My ball's gone over the hedge", she cried.

"I'll go", said M helpfully, "Then can I have some toast?"

"Of course", replied Mum.

M went next door to Mrs. Spooner's knowing full well the ball was gone forever. He knocked on her door, waited, but no answer, but could hear the dog barking from behind the house.

Upstairs, Mum looked out of M's bedroom window into Mrs. Spooner's garden to the right. There on the lawn was the football, with Mrs. Spooner on all fours staring at it and barking frantically!

Printed in Great Britain
by Amazon

35216916R00061

THE GREEN EYED MAN

AJ Bates

To everyone I have ever known

AJ BATES

The Green Eyed Man

Chapter One

The moon appeared and then disappeared behind the grey clouds that wrapped around the sky on a wet and windy evening. The rain hadn't stopped for more than a week now. The small town was under a dark cloud, leaving the streets deserted as most people stayed inside to avoid a lashing. The streets were paved with a darkness that made them seem unhabitable. Hardly a soul stirred in the whole street. Every window was blackened as people daren't face the storm. There were a few sporadic lights shining at the bottom of the road, they were very dim though. It was The Rover Inn. The pub stood firm amongst the onslaught of rain and wind which battered the structure relentlessly. Upon passing the wooden decrepit doors was the bar. It was shiny, you could almost see your reflection in it. Mainly attributed to the liquid it was coated in than its cleanliness. It was sparsely populated, a mere three men keeping the barman company that night. The pub had the smell of unwashed leather and was seemingly dowsed in beer. It was like someone had come and sprayed hard liquor from side to side, front to back. To the right of the bar, there was one man sitting alone at a table; to the left was the same. Sitting on a stool at the bar itself was another man, occasionally passing conversation between himself and the barman. He seemed to enjoy the company the barman gave him. Often, he'd be seen sitting there cheerfully harassing anyone who dared come close enough.

The time was nearing eleven on a Wednesday night, when a dreary, haggard and awfully wet middle-aged man staggered in. He looked like he hadn't washed for days with his unkempt hair and beard. He had a strong looking face from what could be seen of it and his clothes were clearly a few years out of date. He walked in as if he'd just been to war with a thousand drops of rain.

Every footstep sounded heavy; the water had clearly settled in the heels of his boot. He seemed to be carrying a handful of paper which had visibly succumbed to the rain. They seemed barely able to stay together, some pages clinging on to the binding for dear life. He pulled up a stool next to the bar and ordered a double scotch. He clearly wanted something heavy. The man sitting next to him gave him a glancing stare, one of disdain one might add.

"Tough day?" inquired the man. Observing him move the glass in a circular motion, causing the liquid to gather momentum around the walls of the glass.

The soaked man looked over the man reservedly, "you can tell then." He said it as he glared into the glass.

"Bit of a heavy drink for a Wednesday night."

The wet man didn't reply. He didn't seem to want to talk. The other man waited a couple more minutes before trying again.

The dank smell of beer-soaked carpet filled the room and clung to the clothing of anyone who entered. The man put what was in his hand on the bar in order to take his sodden coat off. The coat clung to him like slime. The other man looked over at what he placed down with a puzzled look, as it wasn't something you'd usually bring to a pub. This man was a talkative one, he couldn't help but introduce himself, especially after the barman stopped conversing with him.

"I'm Marty by the way."

The drenched man shot a look at Marty, he clearly had reservations about making conversation. However, after careful consideration and an awkward silence, he decided to mutter "you can call me Billy."

"Well what brings you here then Billy?" Marty asked with great curiosity.

"Nothing really, just stopping for a drink," Billy replied with a sullen look on his face.

Marty nodded and gave an awkward smile as he went back to his drink. Billy stared at the wet bunch of papers he had laid on top of the bar. He ran his finger along the binding, making a clicking noise every time he did so. Click clack click clack. He seemed paralysed the whole time he looked at the papers as if they had lobotomised him with their contents. Marty couldn't help but take note of this strange behaviour. He hadn't seen such an interesting character in this pub for ages. Usually people stayed as far away from the outside world as they could when they were sitting in there. It would just be them and the alcohol. He queried, "those papers wouldn't happen to be the cause of that helluva strong drink in your hand, would they?"

Billy sighed and said "Yep", in a tone as if he didn't want the papers to be mentioned.

Marty sat up in his barstool and said, "you've clearly got something on your mind."

"It's a biography I'm writing, struggling to get it published at the moment. Driving me crazy really."

"Who's it about?"

Billy took another large gulp of his drink in response to this remark and ignored Marty completely. Marty sensed there was no point pursuing the conversation any longer and went back to drunkenly harassing the barman again about anything that popped into his head. Billy had a strange atmosphere of isolation around him, but also one where he wanted to talk. It looked like he was battling himself against two evils.

This wasn't the friendliest of pubs that's for sure. There was hardly anything on the walls and no slot machines or pool tables inhabited the place. Half the lights didn't work and the ones that did barely gave enough light to illuminate a single table. It was dark and gloomy. Twenty minutes passed and after a couple more scotches Billy went to the toilet. He staggered off towards the left side of the bar. Marty noticed the papers were still on the side and his curiosity piqued. He set his glass down on the bar top and glanced at the papers lying on the bar. He couldn't help but have a look. He lifted the top page up with the tip of his finger and saw the name Mr Walsh. The ink had run quite a bit, but he still managed to make out the name. This roused Marty into wanting to read more but Billy came back before he could pursue his desires. Billy was none the wiser to Marty's indiscretion.

Another ten minutes passed by as the rain hammered down on the roof and laid siege to the windows. The name Mr Walsh ravaged Marty's mind like a wildfire during these ten minutes as he knew he'd heard that name before. After the painful ten minutes were up, curiosity overcame him and Marty spat out, "who's Mr Walsh then?"

Clearly offended by this invasion of privacy Billy stood up and confronted Marty. He grabbed him by the collar on his shirt and hissed, "what do you think you're doing looking at my stuff?"

Visibly shaken by this confrontation, Marty reacted sensing the anger in Billy's eyes, "take it easy man, y-y-you just left it there and after a f-f-few too many it's hard not to be nosy."

After a couple minutes of visible tension and livening up the rest of the room, Billy calmed down, mainly due to the vast amount of alcohol he'd consumed since sitting at the bar. His head spun so he thought it best to sit down. He wasn't in the mood for a fight, he just wanted to drink and drink and drink. He wanted the misery inside his head to stop; he always felt like alcohol could arrest it. The pair resumed their positions at the bar and carried on drinking. After a short consideration on whether to serve these two, the barman knew custom was in short supply and inevitably served them another. Billy was staring at the oak bar top flipping the damp beer mat through his fingers, clearly ruminating. A couple more minutes passed, and Marty gathered his things to leave when Billy, with a sudden stir of emotion, choked out, "the man who had it all."

Not really hearing what Billy said because he wasn't in the mood to talk anymore, Marty replied with a confused "what?"

Billy looked back at Marty. "Mr Walsh, the great man, lived on top of that hill once."

The haze of alcohol cleared from Marty's mind and he remembered exactly who Billy was talking about. Excitedly he replied, "yes, yes the rich bugger who owned half the town. God what happened to him? He disappeared a few years back didn't he?" The memories came flooding back to Marty suddenly, "I remember he was all the rage back then, had it all, the girls, the looks, the charm and most importantly he had all the money." Marty went on for a minute or two reminding the whole five members of the pub about Mr Walsh and his life. He turned to Billy and inquired, "how do you know him then?"

"I caught up with him a few years back, one of the few people who's seen him since he disappeared, I think. Met him in a bar just like this back west. Something about his story really hit me, makes me miserable I can't get this damned biography published. He deserves to have his story told."

"Did you write about what he told you in those papers then?" Marty still wasn't overly coherent.

Billy leant on the bar and picked up the sodden papers which were resting on the side and said, "Yeah I did. He was an interesting man he had a lot to say to me that night." Billy wrote about him because he thought he could make some money by selling his story to anyone interested enough to read it. He also felt a responsibility to.

Marty pulled his barstool back in and sat down extremely interested to hear what else Billy had to say. Billy mentioned how he got to know Mr Walsh quite well that night and bumped into him a couple of times thereafter. He had decided to write about him in his times of unemployment.

"What exactly did you write about?" Marty asked. Upon the finishing of that sentence Billy took another large, harsh gulp of his drink and began to talk about one of the most notorious men who ever lived in Hampton Borough.

Chapter Two

The grandest night of them all. The night everyone wanted to attend. The glamour of the Grand Palace encapsulated the surrounding land as people queued for miles to get into the biggest event of the year. Don't mistake this for one of those teenage 'smash your head against a beer can' party; it was one which provided opportunity and growth. It was for the classiest of the class and it was a gathering of the elite, the people who knew how to get rich and stay rich. They all came together once a year to celebrate their successes and show off who outdid who. If you found yourself inside the Grand Palace, you weren't far short of the perfect life.

The sun blazed down as it was about mid-June. Not a cloud perforated the sky. The enormity of the structure could be seen for miles. It stood so imperiously on top of the hill. It was like a lighthouse, guiding in the rich people far and wide. A beacon of wealth. Entering the Grand Palace left you nothing short of awestruck. The captivating hall was packed with businessmen. There must have been room for at least five hundred people in the hall itself. They all mingled together swapping stories of what deal they made today or how much money they spent. The grandeur of the occasion was impossible to miss. The opportunity the occasion provided was enormous. The queues that stretched down Lavender Grove Hill signified the importance the night had. Upon entering you'd be greeted with a drink, champagne of course. Nothing else would suffice for such a place. The girls with their rather short skirts and flesh bearing tops would offer drinks all night long, bringing them round on pristine salvers, accompanied with the finest glassware one could imagine. Nothing in the Grand Palace was short of breath taking, from the fine art that graced the walls, to the superior glassy swimming pool outside. Your whole field of vision would be bombarded with wealth. But nothing stood as tall or imposing as the majestic staircase in the centre of the hall. It was made from perfect glass and marble that one could only dream of owning.

The immense doors at the top of the staircase glided open and out appeared the man we all wanted to be, Mr Walsh. Alongside him stood two of his girls. He probably didn't even know their names, which they were quite happy with, just being able to share personal time with Mr Walsh was good enough. Enough to make your year worth remembering. To the sides of Mr Walsh stood Digby Morris and Charlie Dacre. His two must trusted allies. They made millions together and were rarely seen apart.

Mr Walsh's imposing face dominated the room. His chiselled jaw and protruding cheek bones were hard to miss. Everything about him was in order. From top to bottom not a thing out of place. His brazen white suit made its impact as everyone's eyes were fixated upon it. His blue eyes pierced a hole through anyone willing to look back at them. It was as if he were drawn with a fine pencil. Alongside him, Digby Morris' fierce stare scared many away from approaching Mr Walsh unnecessarily. His stubbly face and thick eyebrows coupled with his straight-faced expressions made him unapproachable to most. On the other side of Mr Walsh was Charlie Dacre, a smile always plastered across his face when girls and some good champagne were around. His blond slicked back hair and well-groomed face stood out from the ordinary crowd. He looked incredibly pleased with himself when he approached the top of the staircase. These three were the celebrity businessmen, they didn't just make money, they made it look good as well. If the dollar bill ever got a makeover, their faces would probably be on it. That's the impact they had. They were like a three headed money snake; their forked tongues would attach to anything of value. Spearheaded always by the strong presence that was Mr Walsh.

The party went silent as they admired the man who made his entrance. "Carry on people, don't mind me," Mr Walsh bellowed

from the top of the staircase. People always seemed to silence themselves when they were in his presence. He didn't mind it at all. He actually loved it. He felt it gave testament to his great authority.
His command was met, and the party was promptly back in full swing. The jazz band were back in rhythmic flow and the champagne bottles were being emptied steadily. He made his way down the staircase with such elegance in his brand-new black leather shoes and immaculate suit. Every footstep had the chime of money. He ran his fingers through his dark brown hair to check all was in order. Mr Walsh was the tallest of the three, in height and in stature. He stood most likely above six foot two and had hands like baseball mitts. Digby and Charlie followed behind slightly smaller, Digby filling out his suit in comparison to the slight figure Charlie possessed. Once he reached the bottom, he dismissed the ladies and they swiftly left, in a hurry one might add. He looked around and saw all the people that had gathered to speak to him and duly felt a sense of pride in what he created. The Butler handed him a drink. He was the only male servant Mr Walsh had, he entrusted him with the running of the house. Mr Walsh accepted with a smile. He didn't drink too heavily though, unlike Digby and Charlie.

He made his way through the excitable and expectant crowd towards the garden area. He was barraged with queries about his investment plans and what his advice was on how people could get rich like him. That's all people wanted, to be like this great man. Mr Walsh ignored the chorus of questions, mainly because there were too many and he didn't know who asked what. Digby's presence beside him meant people didn't ask twice. He went outside and the sun beat down on his face at what felt like fifty degrees. It was only just before seven and the heat was still relentless. He stood, champagne in hand, took a deep breath, and stared into the distant fields where he and his men enjoyed a hunting session now and again. He raised his glass in acknowledgment of a few people who attended, mainly, Commissioner Terrence, who was perched

on the brick wall surrounding the pool area.
After the sun became a bit too much for him, in his suit of course, he made his way to the large television that dominated the hall just by the patio doors. The horse racing was on and everyone had gathered round to see it. It was common knowledge Mr Walsh and his men loved to place their money on the evening races. They made most of their money gambling. Making money from the comfort of your sofa, who wouldn't want that? It was the 7pm at Dobervile and it was evident that there was a lot of money riding on number five, Benjamin's Dream. Mr Walsh, Digby and Charlie all gathered round to watch the horse run. There were huge amounts of cheering and everyone was engaged in the event.
"Come on you bastard!" exclaimed Charlie.

He was much more excitable than the rest, although it wasn't hard as Mr Walsh rarely showed any emotion and Digby was far too intense to jump up and down screaming. As per usual, the horse placed first. Mr Walsh's fist tensed momentarily until it was interrupted by Charlie jumping on his back with sheer joy.
"Another rack in the bank there boys!"

Mr Walsh brushed Charlie aside, he didn't want any champagne spilled on him. He grabbed Charlie's head and placed it against his and told him to calm down. He said it gently though, not wanting to cause a scene. Mr Walsh always had to do this to Charlie, to give him a little reminder who they were keeping company with. Mr Walsh wasn't angry, he just wanted to Charlie to be mindful.

It was true, these men made a lot of money from gambling, especially on horses. People began to wonder whether they were more than just gamblers. Maybe they had a few friends down in the stables. Their ability to constantly win in the horse racing stakes as well as their hand in blackjack and roulette made you wonder. There were plenty more races that followed but no more interested Mr Walsh and his men. They had made what they needed that night. They planned on enjoying themselves.

"Ah, another win for you then Mr Walsh," Commissioner Terrence said with what seemed a sense of no surprise.

He said this as he came around from behind a couple of well-dressed girls, glancing at them as he passed. He was by far the oldest at this event. They were quite close Mr Walsh and Commissioner Terrence. They'd often be seen together at any big horse event where Mr Walsh's finances were invested. Commissioner Terrence was responsible for the County Park Racetrack which the men would be visiting the following day.

The party carried on in full swing, people occupied all areas of the house, more so in the area Mr Walsh happened to find himself in. The jazz band serenaded the whole evening giving the whole place the scent of class and decorum it deserved. Nothing was out of place all night. Mr Walsh sat outside by the fire on the cushioned wicker seats that lay all around the fire pit. Digby and Charlie were chatting away to whichever girl came close enough for them to smell, like predator and prey. They would court the girls one by one into the circle, get them close enough they could feel the wealth dripping off them, enticing them to want more. Every event Digby and Charlie attended was less of a party and more of a game. Who'd get the nicest looking girl first.

Mr Walsh didn't often partake in such debauchery that followed the other two around. Don't be fooled though, he didn't mind a lady or two after hours, but he certainly wasn't one to be seen as desperate. His appearance meant the world to him. A missed hair shaving would most likely cause an event to be cancelled. Or at the very least, the mirrors in his bedroom would be replaced. This wasn't because of some deep sense of insecurity, but Mr Walsh prided himself on everything being in place. Nothing could be out of the ordinary. He relied heavily on perfection.

Instead, he liked to talk business with his fellows and enjoyed the

challenge of striking the next big deal. The Grand Palace was littered with people desperate for the chance to speak to him.
"Hello sir, any news update on the Long Green Meeting tomorrow?"
"No none as of yet sir, we are finalising a few details later on tonight and when we make our way to the Hotel el Oro, we will reveal them to the committee then," replied Mr Walsh.

This was concerning the financial meeting happening at the Hotel el Oro which was about 80 miles to the east of the Grand Palace. The Grand Palace sat on top of Lavender Grove Hill along with a few other smaller buildings which Mr Walsh owned but often let other people stay in for free, provided they helped him whenever he asked. Mr Walsh attended the hotel every year for the Horse Racing World Series and would attend the meeting to forecast his investment plans and any other relevant news for the forthcoming year. He would outline to everyone where he'd plan on making his income and how he'd invest it. Mr Walsh directed a company called Walsh Incorporated. His shareholders would benefit a great deal if his company was ahead of the game, which it usually was. He had had this company for many years now and ran it with close associates, Digby and Charlie. There wasn't much auditing or fraud prevention around so they could get away with the shadier side of things if they so pleased.

Dancers inhabited the slightly raised surface by the pool and entertained people all night. Most of them were contortionists so people's mouths would gape at their elasticity. After a few more hours of the party, people made their way to the exit so Mr Walsh, Digby and Charlie could make sure they were ready for tomorrow's event. They retired to their bedrooms after the private meeting where all house staff were told to stand well back of.

***

"Wait, wait. What did they talk about?" Marty exclaimed eager to know more.
"I couldn't possibly say, what happened in those private financial

meetings was bound with trust."
Marty signalled to the barman for two more drinks, Billy was in desperate need for his mouth was dry from all the talking he'd been doing.
"So, you're never allowed to speak of what happened in them?"
"No, any meeting that took place in the conference room between Mr Walsh, Digby and Charlie was a sworn secret. Even now, he hadn't seen them for years and he still wouldn't say."
"Why do you reckon that is?"
"I reckon he felt he couldn't betray them, like a smouldering fire he just couldn't put out."
Marty had a stunned look on his face that displayed his interest in the situation. He asked what happened next and Billy replied saying, "the trip to the hotel, that's what happened next."

Chapter Three

"Ready boys!" shouted Charlie from the bottom of the stairs directed towards Mr Walsh and Digby.
"Patience Charlie, we are coming down," Mr Walsh replied calmly.

Digby didn't reply, he just shot a fierce look towards Charlie to tell him 'shut up I'm coming'. Charlie was always like a coiled spring ready to burst when it came to pretty much anything. He was an excitable fellow, he always enjoyed himself no matter what. He was a hell of a hard worker too. Much younger than both Mr Walsh and Digby; he certainly had an immature bubble around him. Charlie was eager as anything to get there and start the occasion with more champagne and more women. He was as keen as they came when a good time was involved. He didn't like partaking in the official business meetings as he found them a bit boring and didn't have as many girls in them as he'd like. He only did it so he could be stinking rich. Mr Walsh knew Charlie had a good business mind, he just had to use it.

They were all prepared for the one-night stay at the Hotel el Oro which was about two hours away by car. It was a trip they'd had planned for a while and was mainly for the Long Green Conference as well as it was a continuation of their home life. Drink, girls and gambling. They were also there to see the annual Horse Racing World Series which usually provided them with a lot of money. No surprise.
They made their way down Lavender Grove Hill and turned left as they reached the bottom of it. They turned eastwards with Digby driving and Mr Walsh sitting in the back with Charlie riding in the front. The journey didn't take too long as there was quite a bit of anticipation in the air for the forthcoming weekend. The chatter mainly focused on Charlie who couldn't stop talking about all the fun they were going to have. If he wasn't wearing a seatbelt his head would have probably bounced through the roof. He was

uncontrollably giddy; Digby was glad he was driving do he could concentrate on the road ahead instead. Mr Walsh didn't mind Charlie's zest for life. He knew he'd be a big name in the future. For now, he preferred if he stayed away from the bigger business matters.

They pulled up to the hotel on the gravel laced drive and stepped out of the car. Charlie shot out like a bullet and entered the hotel immediately. Mr Walsh stepped out of the car and took his sunglasses off to admire the beauty that stood before him. He tapped his sunglasses on the index finger of his left hand as he stared the hotel. He waited for Digby to get out of the car and they entered together. They walked to the entrance with the warm summer sun on their backs. As soon as they went through the automatic doors, Mr Walsh was stopped by Race Commissioner Terrence who wanted a word with him.
"Carry on boys, I'll just have a chat with ol' Terrence here one moment."
Digby and Charlie nodded and carried on their way upstairs to their rooms for the weekend.
"Right this way Mr Walsh", the Commissioner said in a profoundly serious tone.

They made their way through the hotel and out to where the racetrack was. The familiar sound of heeled shoes hitting the hard floor followed them until they made their way outside. They followed the track around until they reached a small building just to the east of it. They entered the building and Commissioner Terrence offered Mr Walsh a seat and he accepted. The room was decorated with plaques of all the winning horses since the year 2000 and was complemented by an array of signed photos of Commissioner Terrence with the winning jockeys. As he sat down, he glanced at the photo Commissioner Terrence had with Mr Walsh and some other high rolling officials.
"No photos of the family then Terrence," Walsh said although he already knew the answer.

"Not in the office Mr Walsh, strictly business flows through these walls." For a 60-year-old man you sure think he'd have mellowed out by now, but it was all still business for him. After a brief pause for the gentlemen to get accustomed, the conversation resumed.
"I assume you know why you're here?" Terrence said sternly.
Mr Walsh sat up in his chair and said confidently with a wry smile on his face, "to make money of course."
The two laughed as Terrence started pouring a drink.
In his hoarse old voice, clearly one that had its fair share of cigarettes over the years, said, "number twenty-one will be winning today sir."
The way the two interacted with each other signified the regularity of their encounters. Commissioner Terrence wasn't one for playing by the rules and as the Race Commissioner it certainly meant good news for Walsh Inc. The meeting didn't take long at all as the details of the meeting didn't need to go any further once the business had been discussed. Commissioner Terrence liked to speak about business in his office rather than outside because he felt it courteous to offer a seat and drink when discussing matters like this. He also wanted to make sure the other person saw what they were dealing with. After their brief encounter, Mr Walsh tied his blazer button back up and shook Commissioner Terrence's hand.

The door was opened for Mr Walsh and he made his way back around the racetrack, admiring the care and attention taken to every blade of grass and every lick of paint. He soon walked up the vast amount of stone steps back into the hotel to meet with Digby and Charlie to discuss what the agenda was for that night's entertainment. Nothing was really planned so they were free to do what they pleased. The meeting wasn't until tomorrow so they knew they could enjoy themselves tonight. He approached Charlie's door and could hear him and Digby inside talking. He gave an assertive knock on the door and Digby opened it. Digby greeted Mr Walsh back and he noticed that Charlie was already enjoying himself a lot, feasting on the what seemed like an unlim-

ited amount of champagne on offer.
"Did he tell you the result then?" asked Digby expectantly.
Mr Walsh answered with that smile as to say, 'we're on'. Charlie's ability to listen had been flushed out of him by the champagne. Now it was all set up for tomorrow, they went downstairs to the garden where people had already started gathering ahead of the night's soiree. They made their way down the elevator eight floors until they reached the lobby. The click of their thousand-pound shoes accompanied them on their way to the garden party. The expansive outside opened just short of the racetrack and was full of people talking and drinking away. Charlie didn't fancy much of a walkaround and went straight to the bar area where jets of fire burst up to signal the superiority of the event. Whilst Charlie was buying drinks like the sun wouldn't come up tomorrow, Mr Walsh and Digby made their way to a roped off area adjacent to where he had met Commissioner Terrence earlier. This was the exclusive club. There's the rich, then there's the powerful. This is where the real influencers sat and dealt.

***

"Come on keep going," said Marty in an excited tone.
"Sorry, Mr Walsh never mentioned what they talked about at that table that night. Well he might have done but I can't remember." He glanced at the papers knowing the ink had most likely run on the page where he may have written it down. He was also too drunk to bother looking properly.
Clearly disappointed, Marty took a big gulp of his drink that had been stagnating while Billy was talking.
"He did tell me what they spoke about at the Long Green Conference the day after though."
Marty's ears would have stood up on their hind legs if they could.

***

The sunlight burst through a gap in the curtain and landed on Charlie's face like an unwelcome guest. Last night's get together was still coursing through his bloodstream. Just down the hall Mr Walsh had already been awake for a couple of hours preparing

for the Long Green Conference and the Horse Racing World Series to sign off the weekend. He ran through his mind what to say to his shareholders and fellow investors. He knew he needed their continued support to carry on his successful business portfolio. Digby entered the room without a knock and startled Mr Walsh.
"Bloody hell Digby you scared me."
"Sorry, sir. Not nervous, are you?" Digby asked cautiously.
Mr Walsh scoffed at such a claim and merely added you must always be prepared to please people who have trusted you with their money. Digby nodded and they made their way down to the conference room. Digby's face rarely showed any emotion. Charlie did not make the conference as it was a lot better for all involved if he nursed his hangover away from the people they were trying to impress. The elevator chimed to signal their arrival in the lobby of the hotel. They made their way to the large domineering conference hall that occupied almost one half of the hotel. The door was opened by two well-dressed men and the attention of all inside focused on Mr Walsh and Digby.
"Hello all," Mr Walsh said with an air of undoubted confidence.
"I'm sure you're all very excited to see how the next few weeks intend to play out."
"How do they?" exclaimed someone from further back in the room.
"Well, gentlemen," he said rubbing his hands together as if he'd hatched an evil plan. "First of all, we plan to up the rent collection from 80% to 90% in the next few weeks. We also aim to heavily invest in a few up and coming companies further north of here. We plan for them to be greatly beneficial to our projects."
A lot of heads nodded, and a few claps emerged from the back of the room.
"How do we know the locals will accept your rent collection increase?", another person asked quizzically.
"Well, I'm the one who talked them into making this deal in the first place, I am sure they will be very understanding of what we can offer with an added 10% and, well, if they don't, then our good man Digby will have his say."

He said the last bit of his speech giving a gentle tap on Digby's back. The room seemed very content with the outlines of Mr Walsh's plan and readily accepted them, their trust in him never wavered. Mr Walsh was an impenetrable force when it came to business. The man knew a good buck from a bad one just by looking into a man's eye for five seconds. That's how he built the Grand Palace.

***

"So, you're telling me all he had to do was give a little speech and everyone lauded his work?" Marty asked with great wonder.
"Well, yeah, the man's past spoke for itself, how could you argue? All he needed was to provide a little reassurance once in a while and he was all golden", Billy said with an assured tone. "You don't become as rich as him without being good at what you do. The people knew that. All they wanted was reassurance from time to time."
"Keep going, what else did he say?" Marty asked like an over excited child.
"Not much, all those meeting were the same apparently and he could never remember what was said at which."
Marty let out a sigh, he wanted to know more details about the financial meetings. Billy couldn't remember any more about them. He was unsure if Mr Walsh had even told him.

***

The meeting didn't last overly long and after a few more questions and queries they left to go outside and get ready for the horse race. Charlie had already placed their bets last night and it wasn't far short of some people's life-time earnings. They assumed their position in the stands and sat down. Charlie joined them worse for wear. He didn't ask about the meeting because he knew it would have all gone fine. He had his sunglasses on to hide his tired eyes. Charlie's head pounded still but it didn't stop him from standing up, gripping the railing with great angst. Mr Walsh and Digby didn't stir when the races were going on. They sat back with their legs crossed over each other, cigar in mouth and sunglasses on.

They didn't bother placing any money on the 16.25 or 17.05 as they offered pocket change in rewards. The 18.00 was the main event. The sun moved behind a tree and the breeze welcomed a respite from the sun's ray. The gun fired and the horses left their starting positions. More than one gate jammed and immediately eliminated some of the competition. Number twenty-one soon shot out into the lead and never looked back. The mighty stallion raced around the track as majestically as ever. Never once did it's dominating position seem challenged by the other horses. Charlie cheered the whole way it went around knowing the financial gain it was bringing. He was none the wiser to Mr Walsh's real dealing with Commissioner Terrence. Mr Walsh didn't want Charlie to become corrupted, he was young and still had a lot to learn.

Last night didn't stop him when it came to drinking, he was waving around empty champagne flutes as the horse bolted its way around the course. Mr Walsh and Digby didn't show much emotion, but it was hard to doubt the pleasing nature the win had on them. That brought a conclusion to the racing for the weekend which once again saw Mr Walsh and his men leave with their money up. They stood to exit the stand, doing the button on their blazers up and pulling down their cuffed sleeves to reassume their class. They made their way back to their rooms and started gathering the bits and pieces they had brought. Mr Walsh finished packing and sat on the edge of his bed, he let out a deep sigh and looked up to the ceiling. It was almost as if an air of relief filled the room. It was evident that he was thankful the weekend was over, and he could go home and get ready for tomorrow's rent collection from the Submissives.

He exited the room and met up with Digby and Charlie in the hallway and they made their way to the elevator. The elevator descended to the lobby, not quick enough for Charlie's sake as the motion sent his head in all directions. They reached the lobby again and made a move for the entrance. Their car was ready out front, and Digby decided to drive as Charlie posed a rather significant hazard. The car pulled away and made its way back west towards Hampton Borough.

***

"I wouldn't mind being friends with Commissioner Terrence by the sounds of it", Marty said in an excited tone. He swigged back another nasty cheap beer as he said it.
"I bet; the man made everyone around him stinking rich at the sound of a gun", Billy said solemnly flicking through the pages in his hand. Trying to see if much of it was salvageable. By now Billy was just speaking from his memory of what he'd written.
"Nasty man though. The man saw his family like once a month. Don't get me wrong, apparently, he loved his wife and kids, but they bored him. They didn't give him the thrill the horses or business gave him. These parties that Mr Walsh would throw, he would be the first one there."
"How did she put up with that though?"
"Money. He paid her to shut her moaning and then she would leave him at peace to do what he wanted."
Billy's throat ran dry again and the two ordered in more drinks as Marty asked, "what's rent collection and who are the Submissives?"

Chapter Four

Monday was often a rest day for the men as their party lifestyle on the weekend needed some time to leave their system. Especially for Charlie. He didn't wake from his slumber until mid-afternoon at which time Mr Walsh was sitting on a sun lounger accompanied by a margarita and some nuts. He didn't often drink much when business matters were at stake, but he still liked a day off. He appreciated sitting and enjoying the outside from time to time as it provided a welcome break from the hustle and bustle that business days had in abundance. His eyes set upon the vast fields that backed off from the Grand Palace where many an animal would graze. He wasn't a fan of animals. He didn't see their purpose apart from being game. It was a vast landscape which never seemed to end; he enjoyed it. He felt it summed up his business ventures. They had no horizon.

Digby had probably been awake since six in the morning as he hardly ever slept. He felt there was no time to rest in the world we live. It was go, go, go. Be first or be left behind. He would be found in the gym on Mondays, most of the day he'd be hitting a punching bag relentlessly working on his body shot hook. His muscular figure burst through his tank top. He enjoyed working hard and releasing all the energy of the week into the bag. He felt it was what he needed to keep his composure in meetings. People really did piss him off in the most part. If they didn't provide value he didn't want to know. He had no time for personals. It was also needed as tomorrow was Tuesday, which sometimes meant Digby had to get imposing towards the locals. He would spend hours down in the gym lifting weights and busting a gut. The gym was the darkest place in the house too. Digby enjoyed the darkness down there. He felt no one could see his aggression.

Charlie's Monday's often consisted of absolutely nothing but sleep. Often the laziest in the house as the others would say but it didn't bother him. He enjoyed not doing anything and earning money. Mr Walsh saw something in Charlie, hence why he kept him around. He felt like he would become an asset in the future despite his lavish lifestyle. As for Digby, the fire in his eye frightened Mr Walsh sometimes. He knew if it was well directed, he'd achieve great things and had done so for years now. He'd known him for years; they'd met in business school and had been close ever since.

Charlie came downstairs and lit a cigar next to Mr Walsh. He was still clearly tired from the weekend. Mr Walsh looked at Charlie and said, "will you be ready for tomorrow?" Charlie looked at him and said, "yeah I will be." Mr Walsh knew he was annoyed because he had never been allowed to take part in the rent collection. "Sorry Charlie, you know I can't let you get involved just yet." As he said this he stood up from his seat and walked back inside. As he walked around the corner, The Butler passed him. "Hey, you." Charlie beckoned The Butler over. "What do you know about rent collection?" This was probably the first time in years The Butler had been asked a question and not been given an order. "Well, I shouldn't say sir." Charlie promised not to tell anyone. After looking around to see if any of the other men were around, The Butler sat down in the seat that Mr Walsh just vacated and told Charlie some stories he'd heard.

It was grey. It was always grey. Everything was grey. Nothing livened this place up. Lower Hampton was always in the shadow of its famous big brother, Hampton Borough. Living and working in this town wasn't pleasant but it was necessary. Everyone was brought up told they have to work to survive. But no one ever told you to enjoy what you do. This was certainly the mindset down there. Work until you die and any morsel of fun, cherish it, because it definitely wasn't the norm. The norm was misery. You were programmed to believe everything you were told and to question nothing. When the elites from the top of the hill tell you something, you believe it. When they tell you to do something, you do it. Only one type of person lives in Lower Hampton, the Submissives.

It wasn't always like that down there. There once lived a community in harmony, one which was unbothered by the outside world. They worked hard still, of course they did, any man would to aid his family. But they had fun because they didn't care about money. Money is what rotted the town away and made it into the swamp it is today. One man was responsible. Mr Walsh.
He had a vision in his early twenties to become rich. He was handcuffed being poor and felt his wings to life had been clipped. Money was the only key that could release him. His unique skills at a blackjack table and his eye for a winning horse allowed him to start his journey. After a couple years of winning big and making it large, he couldn't control himself. He met people who made him more powerful and hungrier for more. He was diseased. He also had an amazing way with words. A wordsmith. He was able to convince a man to do whatever he said. It was said once he managed to convince a man to kill his dog because it was making him poor. When he realised this great power he had, he decided to convince people to give him their money. He would say that he'd return it to them double the size. Of course, this was never going to happen. Obviously, he doubled it in size down the bookies and wherever else he could spin ten or ten thousand dollars. It wouldn't be unreasonable to think why people would want to keep giving him their money. The answer to that question is hope. The hope that another man could make them ten times richer than they could ever be on their own volition.

One of the first men to ever succumb to Walsh's scheme was Ronnie Edwards. He crafted shoes from dawn till dusk. Every waking minute of sunlight he would be at his table sewing and gluing. When Mr Walsh talked to him about his scheme his mind lit on fire thinking about what he could do with his riches. Originally, Mr Walsh only asked for about 10-20% of Ronnie's wages. Ronnie was stable enough to give it to him. It's said from that moment on

Mr Walsh went door to door with his idea. After about a month of slow increases, Ronnie was running out of money and hadn't received the promised returns. Ronnie asked Mr Walsh why this was the case. Mr Walsh's friendly face asked Ronnie if he'd like to cash in now or wait for his account to build. Ronnie asked for it now, growing annoyed at the lack of money in his pocket. Mr Walsh beckoned him over to his car and opened the boot. As the boot opened the driver's side door opened. A stocky, stubbly man got out. It was Digby. He walked towards Ronnie grabbed him by the head and drove a knee into his skull. Ronnie's nose was completely busted, and blood flowed out of it at a steady pace. Ronnie screamed, "what the fuck did ya do that for!" Digby shushed Ronnie and said if he screamed again his tongue would be removed. Ronnie instantly cowed and gave up his fight. Digby whispered in his ear, "if you tell anyone about this, I'll have you taken care of." Ronnie vowed his silence. He now takes residence on the streets of Lower Hampton. People are too frightened to let him in their house in fear of what might happen to them. Knowing his and Digby's tactics worked, it was easy from then on to keep doing what they were doing. Word obviously got out about Ronnie and people daren't try and walk the same path as him. They'd hand over whatever they could to Walsh Inc. As for the name of Walsh Inc, it was just a way of adding a sense of professionalism to the work. They termed the operation as rent collection and would do it every Tuesday.

Mr Walsh erected massive factories down there which were responsible for the clouds that cover it. They pumped out smoke every waking minute. He said they were for sustaining the life in Hampton Borough. The hard work down there transposed to the wealth up here.

Before The Butler could carry on any further, Digby came back outside. He gave a strange look towards Charlie and The Butler, wondering why they were conversing. "He was just asking what I wanted for dinner," Charlie said in a reassuring tone, saving himself and The Butler any more questions.

The sun rose spectacularly and burst through the spotless windows and illuminated the whole house. It was Tuesday, which signalled rent collection day. Mr Walsh, Digby and Charlie gathered into the Cadillac sitting on the driveway and made their way down the vast hill on which the Grand Palace sat. They would pass well-kept trees and shooting ranges until they reached the bottom, where they would head straight ahead towards Lower Hampton. The drive didn't take long as it was only a short trip down to the bottom of the hill. By car, maybe five to ten minutes, dependant on the driver. The road was accompanied by lovely almost hand trimmed grass. It was a picture to behold travelling down the hill. Its beauty was kept by local gardeners who stayed in the working quarters of the Grand Palace as payment for their work.

This was Digby's favourite day of the week, collecting the weekly rent from the Submissives in the town. The Subsmissives were the meek, voiceless people who populated the town in Lower Hampton. They were the factory that built the Grand Palace that lay so majestically on the hill. The elites would never make contact with the Submissives unless it brought financial gain, which Tuesday did. There were stories about the Submissives and what they'd do in their spare time. Far too grotesque for men like Mr Walsh to contemplate. They were often seen as dirty and disease ridden just because they didn't have more than one pair of shoes.

They reached the grey run down-town of Lower Hampton where they were greeted by a stench only the poor people could make. There was a rusty fence which guarded the town, mainly to keep people in than out. The gate had been opened and the terrain turned cobbly, the Cadillac gathered dust on its chassis as it traversed its way along. The well paved roads felt like they were a mile away now. Continuing the journey through the town they reached the layby where they parked the car, making sure it was as far away from the locals possible.

"Stay by the car Charlie," ordered Digby as he didn't want anyone playing fast and loose with it. Charlie never went into the town to collect rent; Digby said it was for the protection of the car, but he knew they thought he was too young. Mr Walsh and Digby walked confidently into the centre where the locals waited to hand over their money to Walsh Inc.

"Hello everyone, thank you for gathering here again today. I'd like to say that the rent collection has been increased to 90% of wages. We thank you for your understanding and patience."
There wasn't even a single groan in the whole place when Mr Walsh said that. It was substituted by a mood of acceptance. One by one the crowd came up to Digby to give him the majority of their wage which Walsh Inc promised to grow financially over the coming months. They lined up in the dirt, most people were shoeless and terrified. It started to rain heavier, two Submissives ran over to hold umbrellas over the two men. This was usual practice for the town. They'd been doing this for a while now. They agreed to it in the first place because they wanted what Mr Walsh could promise. The Grand Palace towered over Lower Hampton. The Submissives could see it day and night. It was like a money god hanging over them, begging them to do what they could to be the same. It was almost as if it hypnotised them.
All was well as usual until one Submissive handed Digby a rather light hand.
"Where's the rest of it?" Digby enquired harshly.
The man replied "I-I-I need to keep some more this week sir we just had a baby and need more food." Digby, completely unmoved by this story, asked the man to show him his area so he could see for himself.
The collection was halted while Digby and the man made their way around the corner to see if the man was being truthful. Digby turned back to see if they were out of sight of the collection area and as soon as they were, he pushed the man against the wall and

laid a heavy blow to his sternum. Digby's tongue hung out of his mouth like a cheetah who'd just caught its dinner. He couldn't care less about the man's financial and family situation. He had to pay his way.
"Do you want more money in the future?"Digby spat in his ear. He pointed at the Grand Palace as he did so.
The man, clearly shaken by the events, couldn't find the words to reply because Digby's punch took all the air out of him. All he could do was bring some more money from his pocket and hand it over to Digby. His hand shook violently as Digby took the money. He made his way back to the collection point, shortly after connecting a kick to the man's head, rendering him unconscious.
"All sorted?" Mr Walsh asked Digby.
"Yes, we came to an arrangement," Digby replied with a great smirk on his face.
The collection carried on whilst the wind blew, and the skies became greyer. The sun never seemed to make its way this far down the hill and was constantly buried under a cloud. It wasn't the biggest place. The housing areas spanned quite a far way eastwards, but the centre of the town was very small and lacked any imagination. It housed many stalls which the workmen plied their trade and had factories forming a semi-circle to the west side of it. The rest of the place was just housing. From where the men stood, they were facing a row of houses which stood in front of vast wasteland behind.

***

"So people would just hand over money without any guarantees?" asked Marty puzzled.
Billy looked down at his drink and said, "yeah, they slummed it most of their lives and the promise of being rich led them to believe whatever was told to them."
The wind banged against the door and caused both men to look back in interest. They decided to order more drinks in as they didn't see themselves encountering that weather quite yet.

"Submissives had no heart left in them. The creativity and thirst for life's finer pastures had been sucked up by Walsh Inc. There was nothing left for them but to trust everything these guys told them." Billy stopped momentarily as a bolt of lightning caused the lights to flicker. "Imagine if you had all this extreme wealth slapped around your face every day. That massive palace hanging over you. You'd want to do what you could to achieve it. The promise sold to them could help them achieve that. There was nothing they could do themselves, they had to trust Walsh Inc."

***

Countless homeless people lined the streets, but it did not deter the Submissives from handing over their hard-earned money to the elites up the hill. They felt that the promise of a richer future was worth the hardship of today. They also knew that any dissent would end up with a few nasty blows to the body, viscous enough to make them do anything. The idea was they could live like the elites if they trusted them with their money. If they had kept the money or just run away from the town, they still would never be safe from the fact they would most likely end up homeless. At least in Lower Hampton they had jobs to do and a place to stay. The small amount of security was worth giving Walsh Inc the money. Their hope had been stripped from them a long time ago and the bravery required to move out west to start anew had been missing for years. They knew as long as they lived in Lower Hampton, they'd be confined to adhering to the rent collection policy.

All the money had been collected and Mr Walsh thanked all the people that abided by the rules. He never got his hands dirty himself. He just wanted to be there to be the figurehead of it all; he wanted to show the township he was serious about their money. It was all an act of course. He couldn't care less what happened to the people down in the town as long as they did what they were told and didn't pose any problems.

"All done then guys?" Charlie asked plaintively, wanting to go home as staying by the car didn't provide him with much joy.

He opened the back door so Mr Walsh could get in away from the harsh climate and Digby strode to the driver's side and pulled away at great pace. The car pulled out of the layby and made its way back up the hill towards the Grand Palace.

Chapter Five

After a week of deals and much business-related jobs, it was Tuesday again. Nothing spectacular happened in the week that passed, just business as usual. The men rolled out of the Grand Palace with Digby driving; a massive grin plastered his face as he drove down the winding hill path. They seamlessly drove down the smoothly paved road to the bottom of the hill where they carried on straight as usual towards the town. They reached the layby where they parked the car and, as usual, Charlie stayed by the car whilst Mr Walsh and Digby walked to the collection point where the crowd was gathered ready to pay their dues. Collection ran as normal, everyone abiding by the rules that were put in place, much to the dismay of Digby.

During the collection, a sudden gust of wind blew a couple of dollar bills from Mr Walsh's hand. Digby didn't notice it, so Mr Walsh calmly walked following it as it swam through the air. He made sure no Submissive tried to snatch it. He followed it until it came to a stop. He looked up after he had picked up the notes and spotted a young lady in a green dress reading a book. He looked through the window from a far whilst Digby continued to collect the money from the Submissives.
Digby looked at Mr Walsh surprised, bewildered he would subject himself to such poverty that lay within the town. He knew he must have had reason to go where he went so carried on with what he was doing. He clambered his way through the harshly cobbled ground that ran its way through the town with spots of rain covering his hair. He made his way past the fishmonger and felt himself doused in a raw stench of tuna. After that, he needed to walk past the town's barn where there were a couple of horses amongst other animals. The smells infiltrated Mr Walsh's nose but he continued to make his way over towards the woman's house. He had no intention of stopping despite the horrors that exposed themselves to him. He finally reached a point where she

was in full view and he was mystified over how her beauty effortlessly emanated around her. There was an aura of glamour that encased her, it was like an oasis in the desert. He stopped for a minute, unable to take his eyes off her, wondering who she was and why she was in a town like this. He felt she should be living the life at the top, or at the very least, the other side of the hill, but he knew there must be a reason for her to be down here.

He noticed the door was open and made his way towards it. He took this as a sign and he leant on the wooden door frame, his left hand placed on it whilst his right-hand scratched the back of his neck with nerves. He had been at the door less than ten seconds when she looked up from the book she was reading and noticed him in the doorway.
"Can I help you sir?" she asked tentatively but without worry. Mr Walsh had a trusting face, so she needn't fret.
Mr Walsh was surprised by her question despite standing in her doorway. He bumbled the words around in his mouth until he finally spat out, "n-n-nothing, I've just never seen you before I was wondering how long you'd been out here?"
"I've been here about five days Mr...", she left the sentence hanging as she waited for him to say his name.
"Walsh," he cried out.
"Well, Mr Walsh, I moved here from out west where I used to tend to the animals with my father."
"Why did you make the move then?" he asked inquisitively.

After a momentary pause where she thought whether it was irresponsible to tell a stranger this information, she looked at him and said, "you see, my father died a month ago, he wasn't very well and finally passed away, and a couple days after he left this wonderful earth, these men, these savages, came and ransacked the whole farm, they killed all our animals and took what they could," she said it with great angst and emotion. "I came here because they said great riches were promised out here and I am in great need."

Mr Walsh knew who she was referring to when she said this. Him.
"Yes, we do promise that out here, great riches for all." She perked up at him saying that.
"Well how does one go about acquiring this?"
"Hard work," he replied, and before he could say anymore, he heard a cry from Digby.
"Mr Walsh we're done here." He took one more glance at the woman from the doorway and nodded his head as he left the door. He banged his head on the short door frame as he exited.
He trampled back to the car where Digby and Charlie were waiting and got in rather wet and confused. Digby looked in the rear-view mirror at Mr Walsh with one eyebrow raised, "everything okay? Who did you see back there? Did you get their money?" Slightly annoyed by the amount of questions thrown at him, he nodded in the affirmative.
Mr Walsh looked back through the rear window and looked at the woman's house with a great deal of novelty. He wasn't sure how he felt about his encounter with her. Digby noticed the absentness in Mr Walsh's eyes but didn't bother to question what he was looking at. For the rest of the journey up the hill, Mr Walsh couldn't help but think of the woman's beauty and wondered how he could find out more.

***

"Why did Digby care about what Mr Walsh felt anyway?" Marty enquired.
"Apparently, because Mr Walsh was a man his emotions were irrelevant. All that he should be thinking was 'how much money have we taken today.'"
"Surely the guy can have a girl?"
"Digby apparently thought women were a disease. There to take and not give. He couldn't trust a girl as far as he could throw one. They hindered the process and made a man's life far too difficult."
"Gee, I hope Mr Walsh goes back again, she sounds mighty fine!" Marty said a bit too excitedly.
The weather continued to worsen; the pub was almost their new

home for the night. The barman extended the last call, he too, interested to hear what they were talking about.

***

Mr Walsh woke up the next day with only one thought on his mind, what was that girl's name. He realised he never asked, and her face was plastered all over his consciousness since he met her at yesterday's collection. His dreams had been saturated with images of her. It was a big day for Walsh Inc as they had important meetings with shareholders from across the country. Usually, it posed no bother to Mr Walsh, these meetings, because nothing was ever wrong with his business or his clients. But today he just could not focus on the meeting.
"What's wrong sir?" enquired Charlie.
"Nothing, Charlie, I just had a bad night's sleep."
"Will you be ready for the meeting later then?" Digby asked abruptly in a no-nonsense tone.
Mr Walsh, clearly irked by this, responded to Digby saying, "You can take care of it can't you Digby?"
A bit shocked by Mr Walsh's ferocious tone he answered quaveringly, "yes."
"Good I can go and rest then."
Digby and Charlie went to the meeting in the car and left the Grand Palace at speed. The Grand Palace was remarkably quiet as it was rare he was in it without his fellows. It was quite lonely by himself. He went to lay back in his large king-sized bed that was laced with expensive linen and headed by a plethora of pillows. He placed both hands behind his head and stared at the ceiling. He felt awfully irritable and now slightly guilty at the way he spoke to Digby. He just could not shake her face from his mind. The beauty she possessed struck him like nothing else before. He'd had vast quantities of women in his bedroom over the years and none made him want to ask their name. The image of the green dress she was wearing stuck like a limpet on his brain. And one thing for sure, she didn't belong down in Lower Hampton.

He wrestled with his emotions until he could no longer bare not knowing anymore about this woman. He swiftly threw on a shirt and trousers. He didn't even take a shower or wait for someone to iron his shirt he just left. He stepped a foot outside the Grand Palace where he was greeted with the summer's sun and it accompanied him until he reached the glum town. The Butler watched as Mr Walsh left to go down the hill in a haste.

He decided to walk this time because he didn't want one of his expensive cars turning up down there on a day it wasn't supposed to. He also didn't want to leave it unattended. He didn't know what the Submissives got up to most of the week. Halfway down the hill he regretted his decision because this was probably the first time he'd walked this far in a few years and his shoes certainly weren't acceptable for such a task. After a battle with the backs of his heels, he had made it to the bottom of the road where he headed straight towards the town.

When he reached there, he saw all the people working hard and plying their trade in whatever way they could. He caught looks from the majority of the township because he looked vastly out of place as what he was wearing was far from suitable or achievable for the population down there. He felt his heart start to race and his palms started sweating, he hadn't felt this nervous in years and his cool manner seeped out of his skin quicker than he could restore it. Beads of sweat streamed down his back and soon enough he felt like he'd been swimming. He ambled his way to her house and once again there she was engrossed in her book. He stood at the door momentarily and looked down at the ground, closed his eyes and inhaled deeply. After a few seconds he opened them and gave a shy knock at the door. He could see her elegantly waltzing to the door in a way he thought only a princess could.
"Oh, hello Mr Walsh, what brings you here?"
Unsure of what to say because he was still mystified about her image, he managed to choke out, "how's the work going?"
Pleasantly surprised he had come to ask her about her job and whether she'd found one yet. "Yes, yes after you left yesterday a

man across the road asked if I wanted to help muck out the barn a couple times a week."
Not sure how to react to this as he's never had to do something like that his entire life, he replied with a nervous, "great."
He'd never had to initiate a conversation with a woman before as they provided nothing more than a temporary good time to him. He never had to know them, they just had to know him. She was certain he hadn't come to see her just to ask that, she promptly said, "is there anything else I can help you with?"
After a short pause for thought, he cleared his throat and meekly said, "well I was wondering what your name was, I didn't quite catch it yesterday."
A red sea illuminated her face as she had never caught interest from such a well to do man before. "My names Summer, Summer Green."
"Well that is a very nice name you have."
"Now you've asked me a question it's my turn."
Nervous as to what she might ask, he grimaced as she continued, "Well Mr Walsh what is it you do up on the very nice hill of yours?"
Slightly relieved it was a question he could answer he said, "Digby, Charlie, and I handle our business up there, we invest people's money and return it to them in greater quantities than they originally gave."
Knowing that definitely wasn't the whole truth, he didn't see the need to tell her the ins and outs of what he and the incorporation did. Overly impressed by his answer and wanting to know more she pronounced, "oh, so you're one of the rich people everyone talks about back west."
A slight grin overcame his face and he started to feel himself again and replied, "I suppose I am." He said it rather confidently.
After the conversation, she asked if he'd like to have a seat and he accordingly obliged. He placed himself down on a wooden splintered chair which did no favours to his back. Having not sat on something so cheap in a while he shuffled around to get comfortable. She asked him if he wanted a drink and he settled for a glass

of water to replace the fluids that departed through his forehead earlier.

Now he was sat down he could see Summer with a clearer mind. He looked at her up and down unlike any woman he had before. The first thing to notice were her dark green eyes, they were like looking into a field, a field where he wouldn't mind visiting more. Her eyes were accompanied either side by her brunette hair, it hugged her shoulders with splendour. Her nose complemented her whole face like a little button on a teddy bear. Her lips were coated with a beige colouring that looked so delicate one would have to be careful with. Her petite hands looked as if they could cause no harm. They definitely didn't look like the hands of a farm girl. The way she walked around the house was like she was dancing through the air and every step was masterful.
After she handed Mr Walsh his glass of water, she started to look out the window at the grey cloud that covered her house and her face soon dropped to great sadness. Mr Walsh saw her and got up from the chair and looked out at the sky too, a tinge of guilt crossed him. He knew the factories billowing smoke created this climate down here and he was the reason they were pushed so hard. He could probably build a new town if he wanted to, but he knew that wasn't profitable. He momentarily thought of asking Summer if she would like to come up the hill with him and stay there. He understood this wasn't a good idea because Digby and Charlie would grow suspicious if she wasn't gone within a day. He started to battle himself over her and whether he could risk it. The little voice in his head said to him 'you've only known her a day don't be stupid'; she could be the poisoned chalice! He scanned the house more and saw all the paintings of horses on the walls and how they sat above an array of literature, all which seemed to have been read at some point.
"Are they the horses you had?" Mr Walsh asked with curiosity.

Summer turned around from the window and looked at the paintings of the horses and a tear enveloped her eye. "Yes, that's

one of them, the one I used to ride around when he was alive."
Knowing it was killed in the raid on her late father's farm, he didn't pursue the conversation much further, instead he trained his focus on the bookshelf that dominated half the room. He got up from his chair and ran his fingers across the bindings of the books until he reached the end.
"Which one's your favourite?" Mr Walsh asked with interest.
Still thinking about the painting of the horse she looked down at the shelf and said, "I don't have a favourite I don't think, anything about a story of hope or adventure interests me."
Mr Walsh had a blank look on his face characterised by his mouth slightly open and his eyes unfocused. He knew he never had any interest of that stuff since he was a kid. He thought to himself that was a long time ago now and quashed any resurfacing of those times. He was rich now; nothing should bother him.
While he was stood up, a sudden brushing sensation greeted his trouser legs and he looked down to see a small brown dog had waddled its way through them. He'd been in this house almost an hour and he had no reason to believe there was a dog here. Maybe his infatuation with Summer's face and angelic features distracted him that much. He wasn't the biggest fan of dogs; he didn't see their purpose as they usually stank and needed more attention than they deserved.
"Come here boy", Summer said in a childlike voice and started to ruffle the dogs face like some sort of crazed human. She looked up at Mr Walsh and said, "this is Rusty."

She went on to say how she'd had him for ages and he used to be so very good at herding all the sheep into their pens and used to fight off the meanest of foxes. Completely unmoved by this, he thought why couldn't a man just do it, he didn't lick you or smell and they generally weren't as annoying. The dog glanced up at Mr Walsh with his tired old eyes and moved to brush his ageing body against his. Rusty lay down wrapped around Mr Walsh's leg and looked to have fallen asleep. He looked down at the old bastard thing and thought about kicking it off. Before he could try, he looked at Summer, and the adoring look she gave the two together. It reminded him of the look his mother would have towards him and Eddy many moons ago. He looked back down and, again, he thought back to when he was younger and how Eddy used to enjoy falling asleep near him all the time. He focused back on the dog and gave it a stroke across its balding head and the it stirred and ran back into another room.

His eyes clearly lost focus as Summer asked if he was okay. He looked back at her and assured he was, and he had a beaming smile spanning lengthways across his face.

"Would you like to walk him?" Summer said so invitingly.

He thought back to the walks he'd taken Eddy on when he was younger. Every time he fell out with his parents that's what he'd do, take the dog out. "Okay", he said rather excitedly.

She grabbed Rusty's lead off the top of the bookshelf and tied it around his collar and they went out the back of the house. She opened the door and it backed out on to an expanse of fields. Mr Walsh didn't like the look of the weather but felt a childlike excitement grow on him. Summer took the lead as they made their way across the field.

"What's your favourite animal then?" she asked him.

Having not thought of an answer to this question ever, he quickly replied, "horses."

This was partly due to the fact they won him a lot of money, but Summer assumed he was just being kind because of the paintings on her wall.

"You can ride one if you want, later this week or whenever you're free."

Not really sure how to answer, he muttered, "yes of course."

He felt great that he'd managed to set up another meeting without having to cut past the awkwardness of turning up at her house randomly again. However, he did hope she was joking about the horses. The two didn't exactly talk much on the dog walk. He hadn't been this far out of the Grand Palace grounds without Digby and Charlie in forever. He hadn't seen such a harsh landscape in years. They just enjoyed each other's company until they reached the bridge. On her first day in the town a few days ago she came to this bridge to get away. She said she missed her home life terribly and missed her father and missed her horses. She obviously knew she could never have any of it back. There was something about Mr Walsh that attracted her. Maybe it was his age. He was quite a bit older than she was. She was only twenty-five and he must have been about ten years her senior. She liked that about him, obviously coupled with his devilishly handsome good looks. His maturity and success gave her a comforting feeling, just like her dad did.

"It's quite nice out here really," Mr Walsh said breaking her train of thought. He said this as he admired the quietness of the whole place. It was deathly silent.
"Why does it never get sunny out here?" she asked.
Mr Walsh knew the factories that worked ever so hard around the clock probably did contribute to the climate, but he never really did know why the sun never shone.

As the sky turned another shade of grey, they whistled Rusty to come back over and started to make their way back. As they made their way back it started to rain. The rain lashed down on them and soaked them head to toe. Summer looked over at Mr Walsh and gave him a little push. She giggled as she did it. He slipped slightly on the wet grass and pushed her back. He pushed her a little too hard as she hit the floor. He quickly ran over to her thinking about what a fool he was. He'd just shoved her to the floor! He bent down and looked at her straight in the eyes; they locked together. All he wanted to do was kiss her. He thought she agreed with him and positioned himself full of anticipation. Before he could even imagine what it felt like, she pushed him back to the ground and started to run laughing as she did it. Mr Walsh knew she wanted to have a bit of fun, so he hurtled after her. They were seeing who was going to get back first. They bolted it for about quarter of a mile and by that time Mr Walsh had raced into the lead despite his horrendous choice of clothing.

They both eventually got back into the dry haven of her house and she offered him a towel to dry himself. She had one of her father's shirts that she'd brought with her. She always loved that shirt. It was black and had green stripes marauding around it. It was terribly ugly, but it reminded her of what he was like, a goofy man. She handed it to Mr Walsh as he was clearly soaked and needed to be dried off. Although it was a prized possession of hers, she let him have it. She thought he didn't look too bad in it. They sat back in their chairs laughing away at the fun they'd just had when his watch buzzed, signalling that it was time to go, interrupting the time between the two of them.
"Sorry Summer I must go back now my men will be expecting me to be at home," he said.
"Of course, you go back I am sure you are a very busy man."
He gave her a nervous smile and turned out of the house stumbling on the cobbled path until he finally regained his composure after a few steps. She watched him disappear beyond the shoe making stall and the food market with a hope he would return. He made it to the tarnished old gate and hopped over it rather than opening it, probably due to his hazy mind. Once over the gate he stopped and placed his hands on his knees and exhaled deeply. Thoughts crashed around his mind. He didn't know what to do. He kept thinking back to his childhood and how different it was. How different his life turned out to be.

After a moment of uncharacteristic thinking, he embarked on the journey back up the hill. The sun was soon setting, the sky was emblazoned with a warm orange glow. From a cobalt blue to a jasmine yellow. After five minutes of walking he heard a car making its way up behind him. He turned around and saw it was Digby and Charlie hurtling up the road. They almost missed Mr Walsh as they didn't expect to see him traipsing the hill by foot. Digby hit the brakes abruptly and Charlie leapt out of the passenger seat to open the door for Mr Walsh to enter the back. Digby immediately asked Mr Walsh where he'd been and he just came out with the lame excuse of going for a walk. He also noticed the horrific shirt he was wearing. Digby knew that was far from the truth but before he could question him again Charlie chimed in saying, "the meeting was a success sir, no surprise eh!" A cold front rushed its way through Mr Walsh's body because he'd forgotten all about the meeting today. And then he realised he didn't really care what happened. To avoid suspicion he replied with a contrived, "good work fellas."

The car pulled into the drive where The Butler greeted them and took it to the garage round the back. He smiled at Mr Walsh as he passed. Mr Walsh was clearly not in the mood to talk to anyone, so after entering the house, he announced he was going to rest his head as the sun must have clearly got the better of him.

"I won't be out till morning chaps," he said from the top of the stairs.

They replied goodnight to him as he disappeared behind the doors. Digby sat on the chair in the corner of his room which faced the whole of the room and just sat. He was wondering why Mr Walsh had been off with him for a while and why he wasn't fully focused on the tasks at hand. His face didn't change emotion the entire time he was sat there. The Butler walked in and asked Digby if he was okay. Digby didn't reply and had the same fierce look on his face. The Butler went to walk away when Digby stopped him. "Did you see Mr Walsh today?" The Butler was the eyes of the Grand Palace, he saw everything. The men put him in charge of the female servants that would flaunt themselves around the house. They didn't trust a woman to lead it responsibly. The Butler had seen Mr Walsh leave. Digby was a hard man to lie to. "No, I didn't see where he went earlier,"The Butler replied. He kept it a secret from Digby. He didn't think it was any of his business what he did.

Chapter Six

Mr Walsh awoke with a beaming smile plastered across his face after his encounter with Summer yesterday. He knew he couldn't resist but to go down to see her again soon. They had already set up a plan for later that week, he intended on acting on it soon. Despite the wavering childhood memories that had played on his mind yesterday he just wanted to see her. He sat up in his bed and swung himself around and sprung up like a jack in the box. He washed himself and threw on his clothes again, but this time made sure he was a bit more respectable. He wanted to impress her today for some reason. He didn't know why, but he felt the need to.

He knew Digby would be a problem and would ask questions like he did yesterday on why he was walking up the hill instead of driving. He could tell Digby had suspicions whether he was still focused on work and making money as he should be. Digby liked to dig around for answers. He never liked not knowing the full story. Mr Walsh knew there wasn't much to be done today business wise, so he took a casual morning and didn't leave his room until just gone ten. As soon as he left his bedroom, he heard voices coming from downstairs in the theatre room, and as he approached, he saw Commissioner Terrence and Digby having a spot of late breakfast, brunch if you please. A startled look covered Mr Walsh's face.
"Ah hello Mr Walsh", Commissioner Terrence said with great surprise, as if he didn't expect him to be at home. "Digby said you wouldn't be around today."
A red mist now encapsulated Mr Walsh as Digby's deceit at organising a private meeting with Commissioner Terrence angered him beyond belief. He didn't show it though. "Must have been a small misunderstanding", he replied with just assurance.
Commissioner Terrence soon got up to leave and said good day to both gentlemen and was on his way.

"Sorry sir, at the meeting yesterday Terrence asked if he could meet with you regarding more horse racing business, but I was unsure whether you'd be well enough after yesterday," Digby said rather rattled. Briefly wanting to throttle Digby for going behind his back and organising a business meeting without him, he decided he wasn't going to. He felt a sense of calm overcome him, one that meant he didn't care what business had been discussed. He had more important things to do. "It's okay Digby you don't need to apologise it is understandable."

The air was clearly still unsettled between the two; Digby retired to the outside while Mr Walsh had his breakfast served to him, egg and bacon with pancakes to suit. Mr Walsh picked at his food for a good twenty minutes not sure whether his appetite was there or not. He had two problems now, Digby's suspicious behaviour and his will to see Summer. They were colliding like two trains off course. He knew he couldn't let Digby pull stunts like that again, so he decided to make his way outside and tell him if he's to question his ability surrounding business again there will be a repeat of what happened ten years ago. Despite Mr Walsh not caring what they spoke about he knew he couldn't be undermined because that would lead to a tumultuous future. Digby soon understood his indiscretion and gave a nod to be sure he understood Mr Walsh's threat.

***

"What did he do ten years ago?" Marty asked with a dumbfounded expression covering his face.
"He never really mentioned it. He just said it was something that made Digby understand who he was and what he could do."
"Sounds pretty terrifying, still don't trust Digby though. Sounds like he's got a chip on his shoulder."
Billy laughed at Marty's comment and carried on drinking. The two had got through a fair bit of liquor and beer now. They were belching like old men.
"Did he go and see Summer then?"

"Not yet."

***

"When shall we leave for the casino then boss?" Digby uttered to Mr Walsh.

Mr Walsh had forgotten about the trip to the casino they had planned. Mr Walsh and his men loved to gamble. It gave them a thrill. They felt like it was earning money rather than just stealing it off the Submissives. Mr Walsh didn't want to unbalance the focus in the group more than he already had, so he decided to wait to see Summer again. He knew if he still wanted to see her after the trip to the Opazo Casino he wasn't acting on impulse. He also thought she wouldn't expect him to come and see her so soon anyway, so it was a no brainer, off to the casino they went.

He went back upstairs and made himself look a hell of a lot more respectable. The Opazo Casino was no small fry. You had to impress in order to be respected there. They always carried large sums with them when they went there. They loved the feeling it gave them. The cold shiver that bounced between the walls of their hearts as the roulette ball traversed its way round the wheel was addictive. The sight at the ball landing on their number would send shockwaves of euphoria surging through their veins.

They pushed open the large front door and were greeted with a beam of sunlight. The weather had been spectacular recently and it always brought a smile to their faces. Nothing signalled a good day more than some summer rays.

"It's gonna be a good day boys, I can feel it," Charlie said as he inhaled deeply through his nose, picking up the scent of freshly mowed grass. They got into the car, Digby driving, Charlie in the passenger seat and Mr Walsh in the back. They made their way down the hill and turned off eastwards towards the casino in Newell Heights, which lay in between the Grand Palace and the County Park Racetrack. The conversation never picked up. There was a strange atmosphere flowing throughout the car. Even Charlie's valiant efforts of chatter fell on deaf ears.

Mr Walsh's mood changed when they drove past Lower Hampton.

He looked forlorn at the town as they passed it and his eyes followed Summer's house as long as it was in view. His elbow resting on the window ledge with his chin resting on the palm of his hand. He couldn't help but want to see her. He thought about bailing on the trip but remembered there was a lot at stake here. His relationship with Digby and Charlie needed to remain strong as possible for as long as possible.

As Lower Hampton disappeared from view, the magnificence of Newell Heights was upon them. It was a very large place Newell Heights, many of the rich people lived here as it provided 24-hour entertainment, and everything was at the click of a finger. The casino was on the far eastern point of the town, bringing it as close to the racetrack as possible. This was deliberate so many a man could visit both in a day.
They reached the casino in good time and made their way inside. They were all greeted by Manuel, who handed them all a case of the finest cigars that would keep them company throughout the afternoon and evening. The money that was gathered from the rent collection was brought to the casino as a fund to make as much money as possible. More often than not, Mr Walsh would walk out of there with heavier pockets than when he walked in.

The plush soft carpets greeted their feet as a gush of chilled air stemmed from the air conditioning unit. The Opazo Casino felt almost like a second home to them. It was a warm feeling being there as their coats were taken and placed in the cloakroom. However, Mr Walsh was evidently unfocused. He didn't want to be there at all. He'd played his hand on many of the tables and enjoyed it, but he wanted something new. He wanted the feeling Summer gave him yesterday. He felt like he was losing his mind so he excused himself to the toilet. He crashed through the door and luckily it was empty. The restroom was comprised of marble. Everything was shiny and it made Mr Walsh's head bang uncontrollably. He locked himself inside one of the stalls and sat down on the toilet. He steadily controlled his breathing and his heart started to slow; his head also stopped banging. He tried to rid Summer's face from his thoughts as best he could. After he felt he had done an adequate job, he went over the spotless mirror that covered the whole one side of the wall. He splashed water on his wrists and composed himself.

He left the toilet and was ushered to a table where Digby and Charlie were. They were engrossed in a game of roulette. Digby had placed some big hands and had already come up trumps. Charlie wasn't the biggest of gamblers. He did love a game of blackjack though, he felt roulette relied far too much on luck. Mr Walsh sat on the table with Digby while placing a hand on Charlie's back to give him the signal to go and have a go on the blackjack table. Digby noticed Mr Walsh's lack of enthusiasm for the game and asked if he wanted to sit out for a bit. He sat motionless for a second and then stirred by placing money on black. The ball rolled around the wheel and landed on thirty-five. Digby nudged his shoulder against Mr Walsh's as a mini celebration, but he was unmoved. Roulette went remarkably well for someone who didn't want to be there.
They moved onto the blackjack table Charlie had recently vacated in favour of the bar. They sank into the leather stools and played their first hand. The Opazo Casino wasn't overly busy that day which gave the gentlemen the unlimited access to the place they wanted. Still, the place was polluted by the sound of slot machines. Mr Walsh was dealt a seven and an eight. This gave him a decent fifteen. Mr Walsh was extremely aggressive when it came to blackjack and often took risks that paid off, literally. The dealer was sat on a ten when Mr Walsh had to decide to stay or go. He said stay. Digby sat up in his stool and gave a blank stare at Mr Walsh. This was highly uncharacteristic of his play. The dealer unfurled the next card and revealed an ace, calling blackjack. A few more hands went by with varying success.

He barely remembered the outcome of the hands when they stood up from the table. He'd come out successful, of course he

had. But not as successful as usual. This was clearly down to his absentmindedness. He had been away from the game all day. He was clamouring to go home so he could go for another 'walk'.
This had been a good trip to the casino for Charlie that's for sure, he was stumbling around everywhere on the way to the car. When they got in the car, he opened the passenger window and hung his head out the whole journey home, like a tired dog. Digby felt a great fury over come him as he felt betrayed by Mr Walsh's attitude in the casino. He struggled to hold back his anger. He knew he owed his life as he knew it to Mr Walsh. The man had given him the opportunity to do whatever he wanted. But now he felt it slipping away. He felt he couldn't be without Mr Walsh and the thought of him losing his edge made him worry.
He thought back to the meeting with Commissioner Terrence he had organised earlier that day. He organised that himself and Commissioner Terrence wanted to meet with him. He glanced at the rear-view mirror and saw a brittle and fragile man sat in the back. He thought he was just as good at gambling as Mr Walsh and he could easily sway the shareholders as well as him, and as for the Submissives, they were easy enough to handle. The idea to stand on his own two feet more crashed through his brain.
Mr Walsh sat in the back and couldn't help but think about Summer. He thought she must have drugged him because what he was feeling wasn't normal. He had just missed out on making more money in the casino, but he didn't care. He really didn't. He started not to care at all about anything other than Summer.
They arrived back at the Grand Palace quite late after Digby stopped for petrol on the way back and Charlie had to throw up in the bush a couple of times. He didn't bother to go down to the town as it was late, and he didn't want to cause a stir down there. Plus, he was shattered. His emotions had run his energy levels dry and as soon as his head hit the pillow his eyes slammed shut.

***

"This Digby guy seems like a bit of an asshole dontcha think?" Marty slurred out of his mouth.

Billy rolled his finger around the inside of the empty glass solemnly. He had clearly had a fair few to drink that evening. It was as if something was paining him to tell the story. "Yeah Mr Walsh said he was a tough character to deal with sometimes, heart in the right place though."

The two carried on knocking back the drinks with the barman listening intently to the story now.

"He sure fell for Summer didn't he?"

"Yeah, he said he couldn't explain it. One minute she wasn't in his life and the next she was all he could think about. It was her eyes he said. The calming green did something to him."

"Shame about Digby's macho attitude."

"Digby was a tough man, never say die type of guy. Mr Walsh said he knew that Digby couldn't be trusted after that meeting he organised. There was a loyalty there that he could not shake so easily. Of course he could never have imagined what he would do after though."

Chapter Seven

He awoke with a serenity he hadn't felt for as long as he could remember. A calmness enveloped over him. He got out his bed and stretched out his back while harbouring a gaping yawn. He opened the curtains wide and noticed the sapphire blue skies that greeted him most mornings. It wasn't the weather he was thinking about though. It was Summer. He opened his wardrobe and put on the first clothes he saw. He went to brush his teeth and sanitise his under arms before exiting briskly through the front door.

The summer's sun once again greeted him and accompanied him until he reached the town. Once more he made his way on foot down the hill and then took the road straight towards the town. Before he could cross, the cross-country bus sped past. The number forty-nine it was called. He rarely saw anyone get on it as there was no need to leave. Once he arrived, he didn't even look at the Submissives and just b-lined his way to her house. This time he had the confidence to knock on the door and greet her properly, "hello Summer, are you free?"

This time not as shocked at his appearance she gleefully let him in. She was mightily relieved he came back again. She had the most awful night's sleep thinking about if he'd return. Especially after yesterday's lonely affair. She knew they'd agreed to it, but she didn't quite believe it. His strong muscular face and dominating jaw made her weak to the knees. They stared at each other intently, neither one managing to get a word out. Summer finally released the words, "I know you said you wanted to ride the horses, but I don't know if you would still like to. A lady down the road said I can ride them from time to time because of my history of looking after them," she said nervously.
Thinking to himself that he usually bets on them and has never ridden one before, he is uncertain whether to say yes despite say-

ing he would a couple of days earlier. He doesn't want to look a fool in front of her. However, he can't resist the glow in her eyes and promptly agreed to go and ride the horses with her around the back of the town.
"Excellent! Wait right here I'll be back in a minute with them."
He waited patiently in her home on a creaky wooden chair while she went to grab the horses from the barn a couple of minutes away. She returned and asked him which one he wanted to ride and immediately he pointed at the one on the right. She helped him saddle up and he certainly seemed awkward, high upon that beast, a feeling he only seemed to have when she was around. Rusty soon ran out to join them and immediately became best friends with the horses. An unlikely friendship, but then so was his and Summer's. The field around the back of the town opened up for miles. The grass was strawy and dying. The horses slowly trotted out to the barren fields which surrounded the town and made their way to the same small bridge about a mile away. The weather started to turn again as it was grey and blanketed the fields in a glum manner.
"So, you've never ridden a horse before?" Summer said with a smile on her face as Mr Walsh's cool persona had clearly been left behind.
"That bad then," he replied with a chuckle.
The horse's hooves crunched down on the straw like grass as he struggled to stay in control. Summer and her horse, however, seemed to float through the air. He watched with awe as they made their way further out to the bridge. There was a very small river that ran through the back of Lower Hampton. It was probably the only bit of beauty the place had, apart from Summer of course. They made their way to the bridge and dismounted the horses, Mr Walsh clearly struggling to. Once they were down, they went to sit on the edge of the bridge with their legs hanging down close to where the water ran. The water wasn't too deep, but the current was fast. Further from the bridge, about another half a mile or so, was a small town that Mr Walsh had never seen before; it mustn't have fallen in the jurisdiction of Walsh Inc.

Rusty came and settled himself down on the bank in amongst the tall grass. It was windy and wet, so Mr Walsh was rather disappointed he didn't bring suitable clothing, again. The weather was hardly ever welcoming down here because of the grey cloud that blanketed the place. They sat and spoke on this bridge for a while about anything and everything they could. Away from the loud and brash Grand Palace, Mr Walsh felt a lot different, more at ease with himself. He felt like the protective bubble he had surrounded himself with for years finally burst.

"Did you always want to be like this?" The way Summer asked this was in a way where she could sense something was up.

Mr Walsh was hesitant to speak about what he used to be. He hadn't told anyone the truth. Once he decided he could be rich he never wanted anyone to see his weakness. He thought it was pathetic to want nothing else but to be rich. Money governed everything. Every decision he ever took was overseen by money. But for once it wasn't.

"Not really, I used to want to be a writer growing up. I wanted to write about the world we live in. I wanted to write about the beauty of nature and the way the sky would change its colours effortlessly."

"How come you didn't then?" She asked wanting to know more about this man.

Mr Walsh locked his fingers together and started rotating his thumbs around each other, "because I saw the riches of the people around me and I wanted to be like them. The promise of being rich means you are able to do whatever you want in life. Well I thought it was".

Clearly battling himself he carried on. "I decided to start up Walsh Inc after my father died about fifteen years ago. He abused me pretty heavily. He was quite the drunk. When he died, I felt a power I'd never felt before. It was like a forcefield was lifted and I could be my own man. I haven't looked back since. Giving up power would leave me back where I was when he was alive. Anyway, I was tired of jumping from job to job. I went to business

school and I had an idea to learn the way the horses ran and gambled my way to fame. And once you got a little bit of fame its easy from there. Once you get to meet enough powerful people it all lines up. Crooked people are everywhere and they all want to take money from the next guy they meet. Once I was powerful enough, I decided to start collecting rent from the town in a promise to keep them housed and working, as well as returning their money later on, with it doubled in size. Of course, that was never going to happen, well I did double it in size, but I never gave it back. How could I? It made me richer and richer everyday."
Mr Walsh said this with a tone of regret and hurt. He could barely finish what he was saying without his throat closing up. Summer could sense an increasing regret over what he had been doing all these years.
"Why don't you stop then, give them their money back?"
"I may as well move in down here if I did that. Walsh Inc would probably fail, and Digby and Charlie would kick me out of the Grand Palace and take matters into their own hands."
"Aren't they your friends?"
"I don't know, I mean, I never knew them when I was poor, you know what people are like, money's everything."
This wasn't totally true. He'd known Digby at the very start of his business life. He wasn't poor per se, just not stinking rich yet. As for Charlie, well Charlie only knew the good life. His dad died when he was eighteen and his dad was good friends with Mr Walsh's dad, so he took him in at the Grand Palace. They'd hoped he'd learn his business nous from them. Which he thought he was well on his way to doing.
She could tell the life he'd lived for the past years had taken its toll. Once he left the bubble and was exposed to just himself and a stranger, he didn't know who he was. He became a shell, one lacking the confidence and desire he possessed at the top of the hill. Without money, he didn't know who he was.

"Digby is frightening I must say. He's been a good lieutenant for the past fifteen or so years, but I can sense an emotional wall

within him. I reckon he'd kill his own mother to earn another hundred dollars."
Summer was rather perturbed by Mr Walsh's statement and wondered how anyone could be that selfish and greedy. But she knew human nature was for people to be the best. The idea of being second sickened some people. They both went quiet as Mr Walsh seemed to ruminate about his life quarrels and every decision that led to this point.

He was interrupted as Rusty started to bark and become restless, which Summer knew meant the weather was turning even worse. They mounted the horses in a rush as the rain started to pour down heavily. The horses galloped at an excessive speed churning up the ground as they ran. Mr Walsh looked extremely uneasy upon the horse still and as he tried to grasp a tighter hold on the reins they slipped from his grasp. He slipped sideways off the horse and crashed onto the softened wet ground. Summer pulled back on the reins and went back towards Mr Walsh. The storm grew stronger and stronger. As it did, a bolt of lightning crashed into the field and startled Mr Walsh's already frightened steed. The horse became restless and in its moment of terror kicked its back leg, grazing against Mr Walsh's forehead, knocking him out momentarily before bolting off into the distance, leaving a horseshoe mark above his right eye.

Summer realising the potential severity of the situation dismounted her horse immediately and went to tend to Mr Walsh. She couldn't control her emotions. She lifted his head up off the floor and gave him a few slaps around the cheek which duly brought him round. His eyes opened and they immediately locked to Summer's and he was lost in the void of her soul. All he wanted to do was kiss her and he was about to when she said, "before we do, I have a question."
"Anything you like," he replied immediately.
"What's your name?"
Confused by the timing of her question he replied with "Mr

Walsh." She gave him a look which pierced him with guilt as to why he kept his name secret from her. Knowing that the feelings he felt for her were so real and genuine he gently said, "William." This was the first time in years he's had to tell someone his real name and it felt strange when she said it back to him. He felt a shield release from around him and the name Mr Walsh felt like it drowned in the damp grass. She looked back into his blue eyes as he gazed into her green ones. They shared a kiss which made his entire body weak. He felt like he'd let go of years of pain and anguish in one moment. Their lips parted and she looked at him again and said, "why don't we leave this place?"
The question overcame her suddenly. It was an act of passion. Despite their fleeting moments together she felt like it was the right thing to say. He didn't know what to make of her question, he knew that, undoubtedly, it was something he wanted to do, but he wasn't sure it was something he could do. How could he leave behind what he'd built and what he'd achieved? The riches and wealth that welcomed him home every day and that greeted him every morning made his life worth living. That question felt like the answer had changed when he thought about Summer. He'd only known her a week or so and yet he'd never felt this strongly about someone before. He felt she offered all that he needed in order to be happy. She continued on saying, "you have plenty of money that we can live off for the rest of our lives and we can have horses and you can actually learn to ride one," she said with a grin on her face.

Mr Walsh knew all what she was saying was right. He again thought back to his childhood where he wanted to be an author and wanted the simple life, one where he could enjoy the world go by in the tranquillity of his back garden. He could now have all of that, it was in his palm of his hand, he just had to decide whether to close it shut and seal the deal. What he'd been doing all his adult life. Sealing deals. This was one more of them and yet he struggled with himself to do it. He gazed back at her and made his decision. After a moment of silence, he agreed to go away with

her to wherever she wanted. His heart pounded with excitement at his decision.
They ran the rest of the way through the barren fields back to her house with Rusty as the two horses had bolted off to god knows where. Mr Walsh struggled greatly after the blow to his head, adrenaline mainly guided him back to the house. They reached her house and she laid him down on her bed giving him a home-made ice pack to hold over his head. She dabbed the ice pack on the wound above his right eye and the swelling began to go down. She thought it best he stayed the night and as she was about to ask him, she noticed he was sound asleep. She gave him a kiss on the forehead and departed for her rest on the sofa.

She sat on the sofa rather wet and tired. A smile crept onto her face like a welcomed guest. It had still only been a month since her father died and she'd felt terribly out of place since. But now, now she had someone to look after her. Someone who could make her life whole again. The warmth he provided made her feel safe. She knew he'd done some terrible things in his life. But she saw how he regretted them. Who was she to judge him on his past life when all he'd provided her since she'd known him was great care and affection?

***

"She really enjoyed his company then."
"Yep, Mr Walsh said there was something about the two of them together that just felt right". Billy said this in a way which he'd like to experience such a thing. "Mr Walsh said apparently he provided some security to her life which she heralded."
"Nice to see a woman taking a man for who he is now and not his past." Marty spoke as if women had been the bane of his life ever since his birth. "Where did they go in the end?"
"Nowhere."

Chapter Eight

The town was busy as usual with everyone's hands to the pumps, working themselves to the bone. The rusty gate which bordered the town was open. Someone from the outside had clearly come in. It was Digby. His suspicions of Mr Walsh had grown too large and his absence from the Grand Palace last night spooked him into action. He had made his way into the town by foot, as he too, didn't want his presence to be broadcast. He knew it had to be a woman Mr Walsh was seeing. They were the slime that ruined a man's career he thought. Money was supposed to be the happy drug, not women. Digby never saw a woman's presence as necessary after spending an hour with them. He never wanted kids. This was his life; he didn't want to be looking after anyone else's.

He looked around the town for anyone remotely interesting enough to have caught Mr Walsh's attention. He scoffed at the idea that anyone down here could have even made an impact. He scanned the area until he saw a rather young, brunette haired, short woman. He thought she must be the one, she was the only one of slight interest. He went up to her house and noticed she was cooking breakfast. Definitely enough for two, he thought. One of the windows of the house was open and he could hear the conversation brewing inside. "Here you go William," a womanly voice said.
Immediately, he didn't think this was the right house because no one called Mr Walsh by that name except his late mother and father. That was until he heard the reply, "thank you darling."
Mr Walsh, he thought.

William woke with a resounding headache as his eyes felt glued shut and his whole body felt heavy. He slowly arched his body around until he was perched on the edge of his bed. He gradually got to his feet and went to the mirror. He managed to open his eyes enough to see his reflection and was met with a nasty scar. It enveloped most of the space above his right eye and forehead. He thought to himself, how the hell am I alive? There was a knock on the door, and it was Summer, she had a cup of tea and some breakfast on a tray.

"Quite the knock you got there, you're lucky it wasn't worse. I've seen many a man die from that. You're lucky the horse didn't strike you cleaner." She smiled at him as she said it and he smiled back. She was grateful that he remembered her, she thought the blow might have shut down a few brain cells.

"What time is it?" William asked.

"Just gone 930 my dear."

He panicked thinking they must be asking where he was up in the Grand Palace, so he quickly gathered his things and rushed to the door. He turned to kiss Summer and said, "give me an hour, I'll come back, and we'll go, I'll meet you by our bridge." She didn't doubt the words that came out of his mouth this time and hugged him goodbye.

After hearing the conversation between the two of them, Digby couldn't believe that Mr Walsh was going to leave and probably take a large pot of the money they'd earned with him. In his haze of anger he pulled a notepad from his blazer pocket and scrawled, I forgot to say meet me at the Grand Palace, William x. Summer was in the shower so he thought she'd believe that Mr Walsh wrote the letter because he didn't want to disturb her. He thought to himself, I bet she doesn't know who he really is. He took note of the paintings on the wall and laughed to himself. He watched as Mr Walsh made his way back up the hill and waited until he was gone to go on his way also.

***

"Shocking how Digby followed behind and left that note, seems like a jealous man." Marty said as he stared blankly at the spirit selection behind the bar. "He must have really liked her then."

"I've never heard a man speak about a girl in the way he did. He rambled on about her incessantly whenever I met him. He said that on the trips he took down the hill to see her he saw no boundary line between the rich and the poor."

After his throat ran dry, he took another sip of his drink and asked for another. He continued on afterwards saying, "he said that there was something warm about being down in the town. Although it held none of the prestige as the top of the hill did, something about it felt different. The amount of times he'd been down there and not felt a single emotion for anyone who he took money from, was countless. But the warmth she showed him was something different, something you only ever read about." He inhaled sharply. "He'd left his family ages ago and lived with money ever since, the feeling of love hadn't once seeped into his life since he was young. But now, she gave him that, he said he was a damaged man, and the first time anyone showed an interest in him, it broke him."
"Are you okay?" Marty asked Billy.
What looked like he was on the verge of tears, Billy put it down to his difficult day and how it reminded him of a girl in his younger years. As well as the alcohol of course.
"How could a girl make an impression like that so quickly though?" Marty asked in bemusement.
"You see, he said he never really knew the answer to that. It was just something that she offered him that nothing else could. A sense of real happiness. The happiness that makes you want to get out of bed in the morning. Happiness that makes you question whether what you're doing is right or wrong."
Marty thought to himself that he had never felt these feelings Mr Walsh was felt, it made him sit up to hear the end of the story.

***

Mr Walsh made his way back up the hill with a palpable anxiety over what the next stage of his life might hold and where it could take him. The sun decided to make its reappearance on his way up the hill, drying out his clothes which were still wet from yesterday. The walk up the hill felt like it took seconds and he was at the Grand Palace before he knew it. The smile on his face soon subsided as he saw Charlie waiting for him by the water fountain. Charlie immediately took note of the scar above Mr Walsh's right eye, "what the bloody hell happened to you?" Charlie enquired. He looked intensely at it.

Mr Walsh looked at Charlie as if to say don't be like Digby. In the need to not rouse anymore suspicion, he told him that he fell over a stray log on the side of the road and thus fell onto a rock. Charlie didn't think to take it any further although he could tell it was much more to it than that. Why should he question him, it's Mr Walsh? Digby slithered from behind a tree that was nestled next to the top of the hill and blurted out "we were gonna go hunting in a minute do you wanna come with us?" He said it with gritted teeth.

Mr Walsh glanced at his watch and saw that it read 10am, giving him only about twenty minutes to get ready and leave. He saw Commissioner Terrence was waiting in the house in his hunting gear. A good old friend he'd be sad to leave. Irritation consumed him, Digby inviting Commissioner Terrence over again felt like the last straw for their friendship. Mr Walsh knew he didn't care anymore what they did, but he took great offence to Digby's blatant disrespect. He knew he had Summer waiting for him so he should just decline. But he just couldn't let it go. The years of reputation he had built and the years he had allowed Digby to be his right-hand man. The betrayal cut so deep inside of him he couldn't just go running off yet. What he'd achieved paralysed him from doing anything different. He had to go hunting one last time and then he could be free. He had to prove he was the man of the Grand Palace and it was all his show. One last act of greed. He didn't want those two to garner any more suspicion and agreed to go to the fields out back to shoot whatever they could lay their eyes on. He didn't want their last memory of him to be a weak one.

Digby passed a rifle to Mr Walsh aggressively, and then Charlie, and then they went through the garden out back. They traipsed through the small woodland until they got out to the field. This was the field Mr Walsh looked so fondly on from up on the deck by the pool. Mr Walsh and Digby didn't even look at each other the whole way. Mr Walsh looked back and could see the Grand Palace. He looked in awe at what he built, a small tear formed in his eye and a degree of sadness trickled down his spine. This was his life he was leaving behind. He was grateful to. There wasn't a shred of real happiness in the walls of the Grand Palace. It was only Grand in stature. Digby disrupted his moment with a fire of the gun towards a wild deer.

The time ticked past ten fifteen and Summer grew anxious over William's lateness. She knew he wouldn't be late, he seemed so excited earlier. Through her own anxiety, she looked up at the hill and saw where he lived. It was so spectacular one could only imagine what it was like to live there. She opened the door to have a better look and a gust of wind attached a piece of paper to her leg. She picked it up and read it. It was Digby's note. She smiled and thought William must have wanted her to come up there for one fleeting look at the Grand Palace. Proving to her that he chose her over that. Love over money. She decided to make her way up the hill.

Charlie took aim at a fox running about a mile to the west and took it out with a consummate ease. Mr Walsh couldn't help but nervously check his watch and see the time nearing on twenty past ten.
"Waiting for something?" Digby asked.
"No, just checking to see how many minutes it's taken you lot to kill something", Mr Walsh hit back immediately.

Summer reached the top of the hill and saw this amazing structure that seemed to be something out of a fairy-tale. The beauty of it stunned her and the fact that it was a short walk from the town amazed her. She couldn't believe the contrast. She thought to herself, this is what the people must strive to earn. This whole collection business was so they could live like this. She saw the main door was slightly ajar and she tentatively pushed it open, not wanting to look like she was breaking and entering. Her jaw dropped with some regularity as she made her way around the house, she called for William around every corner. She noticed the vast amount of riches strung up on the walls and the reflection she could see of herself through the cleanliness of the marbled floor.

"What are you doing here ma'am?" Summer turned around quickly and saw a very well-dressed man standing there.

"I'm looking for William," she replied.

The Butler knew this was strange. But he also knew who she was. Mr Walsh's not so well-kept secret. He told her he wasn't in at the moment and that she should wait. He could tell she wouldn't want to see what they were doing out the back. She seemed like a timid individual, one who wouldn't cause harm to a fly. A dash of sunlight bounced off the remarkable back patio windows and she saw a group of men on the fields, just beyond a small wooded area. She could see it was William's impressive figure. She ignored The Butler's advice and, in her excitement, ran outside.

A horse made its way onto the field and it was clearly in a struggle with itself, it was hobbling around. Mr Walsh soon realised it was the horse that knocked him out yesterday. He touched the brazen scar above his right eye. He thought, what was he doing? That animal gave Summer such happiness, how could he consider taking its life. He felt the piercing glare of Commissioner Terrence, Digby and Charlie on the side of his head. He aimed the barrel of the gun at the horse out of sheer pressure.

Summer made her way down past the glassy pool. That's when a gun fired. She was shaken and momentarily her heart fluttered. She hadn't heard such a noise since her farm was ravaged. She looked up and saw the horse falling to the ground in a heap. Smoke from a rifle billowed out into the skyline. She looked on in horror at the horse falling to its death. Her eyes trained immediately on the back of William's head; she could see that he was holding a gun. Her emotions battled each other as she felt sick at what she had just seen. She thought to herself that William was not the man he said he was, she thought that this life he lived was more important than anything he could achieve with her. The grandiose element to his life was clearly too important to him. She turned her back on the field and made her way back through the Grand Palace and back out the front door. She hurtled down the hill with floods of tears streaming from her face. When she reached the bottom of the hill she disappeared into the town. She hastily packed up anything of importance and left her house to wait for the number forty-nine.

The Butler was cleaning a glass as she ran back past him. He gave a valiant effort to stop her, but he couldn't. A sadness overcame him as she had obviously felt she had walked into the wrong house.
"What the hell are you doing?!" exclaimed Mr Walsh.
He looked over to Digby who had a smoking rifle in his hand.
"What do you mean? You were shaking like a damn rabbit, so I took the shot."
Mr Walsh was seemingly shaken by the merciless execution of the horse. He threw a punch at Digby rocking him where he stood. Digby aimed to throw one back, but Charlie soon stopped him not wanting to see the repercussions.
"You're a bastard Digby," Mr Walsh exclaimed as he stormed back up to the Grand Palace grabbing a bag, throwing a few bits in there, and taking the car down to the town. It was about eleven now, so he knew he was terribly late and hoped that Summer was still waiting for him. He drove to the bottom of the hill and had to wait for the number forty-nine bus to pass. He arrived at her house and noticed the door was open like the first day they met. He thought she must have left it open for him to come inside and wait. He approached the door and looked inside; he didn't see her sitting in her normal seat. He peered in through the door

shouting for Summer with no response. He then focused on the fact that the house seemed barer than usual. Books, clothes and kitchenware were all missing. He searched the house for anything that might give him hope that she was waiting for him elsewhere. Then he remembered, he told her to wait by the bridge! Before he left, he noticed a piece of paper on the kitchen side. He picked it up and it read, 'I forgot to say meet me at the Grand Palace, William x.'

He couldn't believe what he'd just read. He knew he didn't leave the note there and there was probably only one person whoever would. That bastard Digby. He slumped back in his chair and with the palms of his hand rubbed his eyes. He looked to the ceiling in disbelief that Digby deliberately decided to go hunting. He knew she'd see he wasn't a pure a soul as she thought.
He thought to himself, it couldn't let it end like this, could it? A shallow, evil businessman was what she probably thought of him now. This hurt him a great deal. After what Digby did, he didn't want to be seen as that. It was callous from him. That's what hurt him the most, Summer's last image of him was him as Mr Walsh, not William. All these thoughts raced around his brain. He knew he'd never set her right unless he found her. He looked up through the window and saw the desolate fields out back. He opened the back door and ran. He ran like lightening to the bridge. Faster than he'd ever ran before. As he ran the dark clouds closed in. The Grand Palace faded into the background.

***

"That man sounds like a real asshole, he had everything, he had enough money to go and live his life with the girl he loved and blew it because he couldn't stand up to his mates," Marty drunkenly slurred.
Billy took a large gulp of his drink and placed the glass down on the bar.
"He couldn't face it. He couldn't face to see the years of power just seep away into the hands of another man. A man who he trusted

with everything and who gave nothing back. That one last hunting session he said was to prove he was always the man around the place. That's what money and power does to you, it grabs a hold of you and doesn't let go. It was his house. His making. His craft."
Billy carried on. "Yes, he loved Summer. The week she gave him was the best week of his life. Real emotions came to him for once and she was the reason for that. But he could never get rid of the pull that power gave him. He had to prove he was the man and that he was the reason everyone around him was so successful. He regretted agreeing to the hunting session. He knew he had more to live for than just power."
Billy was clearly quite emotional at the end of his story and exhaled deeply as he stared at the ceiling. He closed his eyes and felt so deeply regretful over everything he had ever done. All of it was a lie to himself. And as he opened his eyes Marty was gone. He looked to his left and the barman was gone. He looked all around the pub; it was all gone. He was sat on the bridge where he said he'd meet Summer at all those years ago. The story he played around in his head finally had an ending. He finally understood his wrongdoings. He had come to this bridge every day since he had last seen her. Every time playing the story back to himself over and over again trying to find answers. He finally had them. He felt at peace now. He forgave himself. And with that, he inhaled deeply, swivelled around on the bridge and fell. The papers he was clutching vanished into thin air. His story was over. He hit the water. His hair got caught up in the current, it parted like loose string. As he floated further down the river more and more of his hair ceased to cover his face. As it did so, it revealed a scar above his right eye.

The doorbell rang at the Grand Palace as there was another party occurring. As per any party at the Grand Palace it was full of glitz and glamour. The champagne was being served and the girls were out in full force. The occasion wasn't to be missed by anyone wealthy enough to attend. It was packed to the rafters once more.

The party paused as the doors at the top of the large staircase opened. Everyone looked in anticipation for the host to appear. The doors were fully open and out stepped Digby and Charlie, girls wrapped around either arm. They made their way down the staircase with great swagger and as they reached the bottom, Commissioner Terrence was waiting and uttered the words,
"Shall we talk business Mr Morris?"

Printed in Great Britain
by Amazon

24134395R00040